LAUGH
WITH THE
MOON

LAUGH
WITH THE
MOON

SHANA BURG

DELACORTE PRESS

Northern Tier Library
Pine Center

This is a work of fiction. Names, characters, places, and incidents either are the product of the author's imagination or are used fictitiously. Any resemblance to actual persons, living or dead, events, or locales is entirely coincidental.

Text copyright © 2012 by Shana Burg
Jacket art copyright © 2012 by Harvey Chan

All rights reserved. Published in the United States by Delacorte Press, an imprint of Random House Children's Books, a division of Random House, Inc., New York.

Delacorte Press is a registered trademark and the colophon is a trademark of Random House, Inc.

Visit us on the Web! randomhouse.com/kids
Educators and librarians, for a variety of teaching tools,
visit us at randomhouse.com/teachers

Library of Congress Cataloging-in-Publication Data
Burg, Shana.
Laugh with the moon / Shana Burg. — 1st ed.
p. cm.
Summary: Massachusetts thirteen-year-old Clare, grieving after her mother's recent death, reluctantly travels with her father to spend nine weeks in a remote village in Malawi, where new friends and experiences help open her mind and heart. ISBN 978-0-385-73471-4 (hc) — ISBN 978-0-385-90469-8 (lib. bdg.) — ISBN 978-0-375-98568-3 (ebook) [1. Interpersonal relations—Fiction. 2. Self-actualization (Psychology—Fiction. 3. Fathers and daughters—Fiction. 4. Death—Fiction. 5. Grief—Fiction. 6. Americans—Malawi—Fiction. 7. Malawi—Fiction.] I. Title.
PZ7.B916259Lau 2012
[Fic]—dc23
2011023879

The text of this book is set in 12-point Goudy.
Book design by Vikki Sheatsley

Printed in the United States of America
10 9 8 7 6 5 4 3 2 1
First Edition

Random House Children's Books supports the First Amendment
and celebrates the right to read.

For my friends in Malawi
And in memory of Felicity, Norman, and Stella

LAUGH
WITH THE
MOON

CHAPTER 1

I press my nose against the airplane window and breathe faster, faster, more, more, more. I try to erase what's outside. In my mind, I beg for someone to help me. *Help me!* I want to yell. But you know, who would? Who could? Only Dad, of course, and flying here was his idea in the first place.

Branches slam against each other in the wind and rain. The jungle is so crowded. How can anything possibly grow in it? My eyes trace a thick vine twisting around and around an enormous tree trunk, desperately trying to choke the life out of it. Who will win: the vine or the tree? I don't like that vine. I don't like it one bit.

I breathe even faster, and by the time the plane jolts to a stop, I've covered the window with mist. Now I can't see outside, can't see where I'm going to be stuck for the next nine weeks. All I can do is watch my father pack up the medical report he's been poring over ever since we switched planes a few hours ago. "Come on, honey," he says, as if he hasn't just torn me away from home, as if he hasn't made me leave all my friends and memories behind.

He tucks the medical report neatly inside his army-green traveler's backpack. I unbuckle my seat belt and stand. My heart thumps, quick and light, quick and light, never touching down for a full beat. While Dad checks the messages on his cell phone, there's a creak. Then a loud, long roar. I crouch and wipe off the window to look for the airplane racing down the runway, about to escape. But I don't see another plane, only forest-green, olive-green, green-gold. And rain, rain, rain.

A blast of heat fills the cabin. The month of January really is summer in this place. Under my sweater and jeans, tiny beads of sweat bubble up all over my skin. I take off my cotton scarf and stuff it into my backpack while that strange roar grows louder.

A dark-skinned woman stands in the row of seats in front of me, her head wrapped in a bright red cloth. A tall, thin girl stands beside her, a younger version of the woman. The girl talks to her mother in a language that sounds like fireworks, full of bursts and pops. She holds her hand over her mouth, giggling. I try not to look at her. She probably has so many minutes with her mother she can't even count them.

I grab the gold heart pendant hanging around my neck, feel the dent that I chewed right into the middle of it. Mom made it for me a few years ago when she took a jewelry design class at the center for adult education. Dad slips his phone into his pocket and gives me a squeeze around my shoulders. I pull away.

"How long are you going to keep up the silent treatment?" he asks.

I check my watch and adjust for the eight-hour time difference between Boston and here. I haven't spoken for the entire trip, not even during the layover in South Africa. That would put me at a grand total of twenty-six hours and thirty-two minutes, never mind that I was sleeping for at least eighteen of them. It's so impressive—maybe even a world record—that I actually consider sharing the news.

But I don't, because that would break my promise, and in my book, promises are not meant to be broken. Not promises fathers make to daughters, like "I'll take care of you" and "I always have your best interest at heart." And not promises daughters make to fathers, like "I will never speak to you until you take me back where I belong."

I follow Dad down the cramped aisle. The rumble grows louder and my breath snakes up my throat. Soon I'm at the mouth of the plane. I realize it's the crazy storm outside that's making such a racket. Cold raindrops prick me like needles. There isn't even a tunnel connecting the airplane to the airport.

A flight attendant stands by the cockpit. "Welcome to Malawi," she says, and smiles. I know I should smile back. It's the right thing to do. But I can't. I doubt I'll ever smile again.

A bolt of lightning strikes the treetops. I'm thinking it's pretty dumb to stand on a metal staircase in an African storm. We could be killed.

But my father? He's another story! He inhales the slate-gray sky like it's full of jasmine, like the smell of this place is a total thrill. Then he clomps down the metal staircase to the runway. I mean, I'm sure he's clomping, but I can't hear his footsteps; I can't even see him very well, because the storm is that vicious, that wild.

When he reaches the runway, he turns to make sure I'm following. But I'm not. I'm not going.

"Have a lovely day," the flight attendant says. "Thank you for flying Air Malawi."

Rain screams down from the sky. Lightning too. Here I am, five years old again, standing on the edge of the high diving board. I suck in my breath and squeeze my eyes shut. *One, two, three!* Then I do it. I run down the steps and wait to be taken to my death—too young and too suddenly—just like my mom.

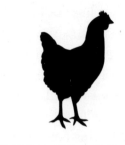

CHAPTER 2

Not only am I alive when I reach the door to the terminal, but I'm also a shivering mess. I glance around.

"Bet you feel like a marshmallow that fell into a bag of dark chocolate while someone was making s'mores," Dad says, and smiles.

I squirm and make a mental note to send my father to comedy school when we get back. He loves to tell jokes, but usually they're pretty bad.

We show our passports to an official and press through the metal turnstile, where an African man wearing a white button-down shirt and black pants waves to us across the small crowd. He holds a handmade sign that says DOKTOR.

Dad waves to the man as our soggy sneakers squeak against the linoleum floor. "Welcome to the Warm Heart of Africa," the man says. "I am Emmanuel Mbalazo, the driver for the Global Health Project. I shall transport you to your house."

After we collect our luggage and change our clothes, we follow Mr. Mbalazo across the parking lot. It's cloudy outside and the jet lag is hitting me big-time, but at least the rain has stopped. Mr. Mbalazo puts our luggage in the trunk and opens the back door. I slide in beside Dad. The driver's side is on the right, which gives me a pretty big clue that everything in this country is mixed up all over the place.

It's a four-hour drive south to the Machinga district, where we're going to live, but after only a couple of minutes Mr. Mbalazo pulls over. "For your food needs," he says. I glance through the window at an outdoor market. I'm not in the mood to shop, but what choice do I have? My stomach is growling. Plus, I'm not going to stay in the car by myself waiting to get robbed. Everyone knows that where there's poverty there's misery, and where there's misery there's crime. I take my backpack off and hold it close to my chest, then slip out of the car behind Dad into the afternoon light.

The marketplace is a quilt of bright blue, yellow, and orange plastic sheets. On top of the sheets are people trying to sell carved chairs, masks, clothes, piles of peanuts still in the shells, fruits, vegetables, and used clothes and shoes. "*Nyemba! Nyemba!*" someone shouts. I turn to see a man sitting beside baskets full of different-colored beans. They are the colors of my paints: gold ochre, raw sienna, and violet. I miss my paints. How could I not have brought them? I can't beat myself up too long, though, because it's almost impossible to have a complete thought in this noise.

The sound of a blaring radio blends with the people trying to hawk anything they can grow or make. And there are kids everywhere, pacing the sidewalks, selling dolls and toy cars with long pull handles made from scraps and wires.

Dad speaks to the vendors in a mix of English and bits of Chichewa he remembers from when he used to live in Malawi. He loads up on strange-looking fruits, bottles of water, grains, and a loaf of bread. Mr. Mbalazo is helping him negotiate a better deal on a bag of nuts when suddenly, five little boys hurry toward me.

The boys are holding their palms open for money. "*Kwacha. Kwacha,*" they say. I can't breathe. I can't think. I can't even see my father anymore, so I reach into my backpack. There's my phone, my gum, my barrette, and finally, finally, a quarter.

Change. I need more. I need some coins for each of them. Their stomachs are swollen. Their belly buttons look like plums. They need to eat. They need new clothes. Where are their parents?

My fingers dive back into my bag frantically, but they come up empty.

So I hold the quarter. Who should get it? That boy with the torn shirt? Or that one, pulling a toy car made from twisted hangers and bottle caps? It's impossible to choose.

Then I don't have to: a small hand pries open my fist and scrapes the coin out of my palm.

"Clare?" Dad calls. The boys scatter.

I'm shaking. How could he bring me here, to one of the poorest countries on earth? How could he think this is an okay place for a kid like me? It's a good thing I'm not speaking to him, because if I let loose the string of curse words on the tip of my tongue, I'd be grounded until I turn seventeen.

Dad hands me one of the plastic bags full of groceries to carry. "You okay?" he asks.

I glare.

"Just think," Dad says, "maybe you can write about it for your project."

I groan as I follow my father and Mr. Mbalazo back to the car. Even though my school in Brookline is all the way across the ocean from here, I guess I'll never really get away from it. Mrs. Middleton, my school principal, dragged me into the office a few days ago and gave me the most atrocious assignment of my life. I have to prepare something to share with the entire grade about what I learn here.

We put the grocery bags in the trunk. No sooner do I get into the backseat beside Dad than I do what I do best lately: I conk right out. And at least for a while, I leave behind everything that's wrong with my life.

When I open my eyes again, the sky has changed from slate-gray to the color of an old bruise. We pass farm after farm after farm, and hundreds of women carrying buckets on their heads and babies on their backs.

Mr. Mbalazo slows down as a herd of furry brown creatures with spiky horns charges across the road. It's crazy, but I'm jealous. Jealous of how they know exactly where they're going. Where? I have no idea, but obviously they do. They have a purpose. A life.

I haven't felt like sketching in days, but now my fingers itch for charcoal. Still, I'm too lazy to actually bother pulling out my pad, even though it's right there in my bag. I want to remember these unscrewed-up gazelles, but since I haven't drawn them, I'll probably forget they even exist. I forget everything these days, like why I used to think my father was cool, why I used to love to read, and my mother.

And tell me, who does that? Forgets her own mother? I knew her for thirteen years, and even though there are pictures of Mom all over the house, when I close my eyes, I can only see her in pieces. Her spray of freckles. Her light green eyes. I don't know what kind of brain damage I have, but for some reason, unless I'm staring at her photo, I can't picture her face whole.

Sometimes I wonder if I have a tumor, because my memory's getting so bad. A few months ago, when I was sleeping over at Marcella's house, I told her I was scared. Being in the dark made it easier to talk.

"Ginkgo," Marcella whispered from her bed.

"What?" I asked from my cot.

"Ginkgo. It's this herb that fixes your memory," she said.

Hope twisted in my chest for the first time in so long.

"My grandpa takes it. We'll get it tomorrow. You'll be fine."

I sighed and looked at the clock. It was already past midnight. In less than twelve hours, I might be cured. I could hardly sleep from the excitement.

In the morning, we went straight to the pharmacy on the corner of Beacon and Harvard streets. I took ginkgo biloba capsules every morning for a week, but when I closed my eyes and tried to see my mother, it was the same old thing: her perfect teeth, her long lashes, her dangling red earrings. The reception was still bad and I couldn't get all of her to appear.

By the end of the week, I started to panic. But when Marcella asked how it was going with the ginkgo, I told her great and thanked her for the excellent suggestion. I didn't want her to think I wasn't happy. Why would Marcella want a friend who isn't happy? Everyone wants to hang out with Marcella—she's the captain of the field hockey team, she's pretty without looking like everyone else, and she's smart—and I don't want to take any chances and give her up to someone like Crystal, who's always inviting Marcella to parties and trying to get her to join the superpopular crowd.

Now Dad takes out the loaf of bread and a bottle of water. "Hungry?" he asks.

I nod and he tears off a hunk. I only manage to eat a few bites before we pass a man with a stick over his shoulder. My stomach lurches. A bunch of plucked chickens dangles from both ends of the stick. *Don't think about it!* I tell myself. *Forget you are here.*

I drop the hunk of bread on my lap and grab my cell phone out of my backpack. I need to text Marcella to tell her what I just saw. I need to send an SOS. I've got to get out of here! I press the power button. I tilt my phone away from Dad, but the words "no signal" appear on the screen.

Did I groan? I must have, because Dad snaps the cap back onto his highlighter pen and peeks over my shoulder at the phone. "Excuse me, Emmanuel," Dad says. "I had heard that there's phone reception in Malawi now."

"Near everywhere," Mr. Mbalazo says from the front seat. "Here in the southern bush, most especially in the rainy season, I do fear it can be spotty."

"I was planning to get you a chip," Dad says to me. "But I guess it's not going to work."

I swallow. Even without reception, I can open the photo of Mom and me at the lighthouse on Marblehead Neck. There are hundreds of sailboats in the harbor. The sun is dripping silver sparkles across the ocean like fairy dust. Mom's arm is around me. I tap the tiny screen and enlarge the photo. I stare at the place where her arm touches my shoulder until the photo turns blurry from my tears.

Dad grabs my hand. "It's okay, honey," he says.

I pull my hand away, hurl my phone into my bag, and feel myself choke.

We drive for miles and miles while the grainy dusk settles in and the colors disappear from the sky. There are no condos. No buses. No restaurants. Just jungle on both sides of the dirt road.

"You shall be home in an hour's time," Mr. Mbalazo says. I know he means well, but I want to scream: *Home? My home is across the ocean, more than seven thousand miles from here!*

Then again, I should say my *house*. My house is across

the ocean, more than seven thousand miles from here, because I don't have a home anymore. I know I don't look like your average homeless person. But that's what I've become. I mean, we still have a house on Russell Street, but it's just brick and wood and plaster now. There's no smell of cinnamon toast in the morning or paintings set on easels all over the living room. There's no one shouting out the questions to the *Jeopardy!* answers on the TV. And there's no one learning to play the banjo, rather badly, while I'm doing homework. These days, when I'm in that house where I have lived my whole life, I feel the wind and chill of winter as much as the man who sleeps on the church steps on Beacon Street.

I wrap my arms around myself and shiver as Mr. Mbalazo slows down the car. I wonder if I'm losing it. I mean, I've been under a huge amount of stress for the last eight months, and I guess I'm finally going crazy. Nuts.

Or, maybe I should say bananas. Because what I see out the window—well, what I think I see—is a monkey the size of a man. A very large man. It lumbers upright on two feet across the dirt road. And it isn't just any monkey. It's a thirsty monkey. It's carrying a can of Coke—regular, not diet.

CHAPTER 3

The monkey stops right in front of us, tilts back its head, and guzzles. Then it crunches the can in its fist, chucks it on the ground, and disappears into the jungle on the other side of the road.

"Ha!" Dad says. "What a world this would be if we could distribute medicine like they deliver cola!" Then he laughs. It's one of those laughs that goes on and on forever, like a jumbo hot dog from Fenway Park. I don't know why hearing my father laugh makes me furious, but it does.

Mr. Mbalazo moves the stick shift into gear again. "This is *chiyendayekha*," he says. "Big monkey."

I grab my phone to text Marcella about this bizarre place, then remember the thing is useless. Instead, I capture a rough image of the gorilla-monkey on my sketchpad, and when I'm done, I glance at my father. His eyes are closed. I'm afraid he might snore. Like most doctors, my father hardly sleeps, but when he does, watch out. For now, though, he's breathing like a baby. I press my finger into his arm. What would Dad think of my little experiment? What would he think of me trying to touch the old him, to see if the part of him that used to care about me still exists? Before I can tell anything for sure, Dad shifts in his seat, so I yank my finger away.

As predicted, a few minutes later, the rumbling begins. When Mr. Mbalazo hears my dad snore like a drunken sailor, he laughs a rich, hearty laugh. Then he says, "Soon we enter the trading center near to your home. Tomorrow you may visit there."

I shove my father hard, back and forth, back and forth, until he burbles, shakes his head, and wipes his eyes.

I look out the window. It's completely dark. I can't see a thing.

Mr. Mbalazo turns off the main road onto a narrow path. I wonder how he knows where to go. There aren't any street signs with white reflective letters glittering in the night. I don't even see any trees. But I do hear sticks and leaves scraping the windows.

Mr. Mbalazo pulls into a driveway, takes out the key, and pops the trunk. "Here you are!" he says. Dad gets out to help him carry our luggage and supplies inside. I stay stuck to the seat like a stamp. I grind my teeth into my dented heart pendant while the sounds of the African night creep through the open car door.

Once Dad and Mr. Mbalazo come back to the car, I get out and stretch and try to lose the feeling that I'm stuck in a nightmare. "Wishing you a season of good fortune," Mr. Mbalazo tells us before getting into the driver's seat. As he crunches backward over the gravel driveway, Dad and I wave into the glare of headlights. And when it's completely dark and creepy again, I follow Dad into the house, which is the size of half a Pop-Tart.

There's nothing inside but two tiny bedrooms, a bathroom, a closet-sized living room, and a kitchen with a small round table. There are no pictures on the white walls, and the overhead lights are the fluorescent kind designed by some kook for places like hospitals and schools. Worst of all, the bedrooms have ugly canopies that are the color of dead fish. And aside from the twin beds with mattresses as thin as bitten fingernails, there's nothing in either bedroom except a plain wooden dresser with three drawers and a window with a screen but no glass.

Dad moves my luggage into the room closest to the bathroom. "What's wrong?" he asks.

Before I can stop it—before I remember that a world record is at stake—a scream wells up inside me and blows right out of my mouth. "What's wrong is that you pulled me away from my entire life right in the middle of my formative years!"

Marcella told me that when a girl turns into a teenager—which I happened to do this past summer—she enters the most important years of her entire life. Now I pass the information on to my father, information I'm sure Mom knew by heart: "News flash!" I say. "In a girl's formative years, her whole personality gets formed." I look around. "In a place like this, mine will get formed deranged!"

"What do you mean?" Dad asks.

"What do I mean?" If he doesn't get it, I can't begin to explain. "Can you take down the canopy, at least? It's disgusting."

"Oh." Dad chuckles. "It's not a canopy, Clare. It's a malaria net. You let it hang around the edges of the bed when you sleep. Keeps the bugs out."

I don't see any bugs. Still, Dad insists that we leave that ugly net up. I press my forefingers to my temples. "And these lights are giving me a headache," I say.

"That I can fix," Dad says. He walks out of my brand-new bedroom and rummages through his bag that's still in the living room. When he comes back, he's got two flashlights. He presses a switch on the wall and turns out the overhead lights.

All of a sudden, everything powers down.

And even though the air is heavy and the house is tiny, I can hear tons of space between Dad and me. I can hear all the emptiness left by everything that isn't turned on—computers and cell phones and beepers—all the things that usually chop up our time together and slice it into pieces so small they barely exist.

Dad turns on the flashlights and hands one to me. "Let's pretend it's night," he says.

"It is night," I say, and follow him through the dark house to the kitchen.

"It's nine o'clock here in Malawi, but in Brookline . . . only one in the afternoon."

When you've been traveling more than thirty hours like I have, it's impossible to keep track of your life. When you've been plucked out of school right when you're on the verge of getting your first actual kiss, you feel cheated. And when you're glad you didn't get that kiss because you don't have a mother to tell about it, then you know things really are messed up.

"Wait here. I've got to get something," Dad says.

Of course, I know he's in the next room, so I shouldn't be having a conniption, but I totally am. It's scary in this place. There are all kinds of rattles, hisses, and hums. It sounds like a spooky percussion symphony. After a minute, though, the thud of my heart in my ears grows loud enough to drown out the sounds of the African night.

When Dad returns, he's got a package of peanut butter crackers, a bottle of water, and a white Malarone pill so I won't get malaria. I put the pill on my tongue, but the second I take a swig of water, there's a horrific screech. I splutter the pill onto the table.

"If I recall, that's the bush baby monkey," Dad says. It's been more than twenty years since my father's lived in this country, but he still thinks he knows everything about it. "Bush babies usually give birth to twins."

"Exactly what I need!" I say. "Some monkey mother giving birth in my ear."

Dad chuckles and goes off to get me another pill. While he's gone, I take three breaths in and out of my nose to try to calm myself down. It doesn't work. I want to yell *Hurry up and get back here already!* But of course, I don't. I can't let Dad know I'm scared.

At least pill number two goes down without a hitch. "Good job," Dad says. And when I finish the crackers, he tells me to get ready for bed. "Remember to brush your teeth with bottled water. The tap water has all kinds of germs that could get you really sick."

I grab my water bottle off the table.

After I brush, I go to the bedroom, where the moonlight is streaming through the window screen. I change into my pajamas and climb under the mosquito net. I'm trapped. Dad sticks his head in the doorway. "Good night, honey. Sweet dreams," he says.

And I decide right there and then that I've made a mistake by talking to him. If I have any prayer of getting back to Brookline anytime soon, I've got to be more disciplined about the silent treatment. I've got to make Dad regret every second we're here.

CHAPTER 4

Sunlight crashes through the window screen onto my head. I'm alarmed to see where I am. I lug myself out of bed, run to the bathroom, then pass Dad reading on the living room couch.

"It's already two o'clock, Clare," he says. "Why don't you grab something to eat, and then what do you say we get going to Mkumba?"

As if I'm going to answer him! I march straight to the kitchen, where I tear into a box of wafer cookies. They make a great breakfast.

"Cut it out, already," Dad says, now standing in the kitchen doorway. "I thought you said you aren't a little kid anymore."

I shrug. I wish Marcella was here so I could ask her what to do.

Dad sits down next to me at the kitchen table.

Suddenly, I'm feeling claustrophobic. He turns over the medical report in his hand and sketches a map of the village where he used to live when he was in the U.S. Peace Corps. "Doubt much has changed," he says as he draws huts and labels them. "Families in the villages tend to stay put." He draws arrows between the huts to indicate who's related to who.

Dad shows me where his friend Stallard lived. "Stallard and I were like brothers back in the day," he tells me. "We exchanged letters for years before we fell out of touch. He used to always ask when I was going to bring you and your mother to meet him. You know, that's why I wrote in September . . . to tell him the news," he says. Dad shakes his head, like if he tries hard enough, he can toss the memory of Mom right out of it. I guess it works, because a second later, he goes back to his masterpiece with a little smile on his face and continues to describe his old pals. By the time Dad finishes drawing, there are about a hundred arrows shooting all over the place, and I can barely keep everyone straight.

After I eat half the box of cookies, I go into the bathroom. Of course, it's hard to see anything in the six-by-six-inch mirror hanging on the wall. Still, I'm almost confident that I've managed to scrunch curls from the nest on my head. I put on my cranberry dress with navy batik figures. It looks very ethnic. It's my best hope of fitting in here.

Next, I open the guidebook that I read on the airplane and rip out the page my father will need about manners, because manners aren't his strong suit. In the past eight months, it has been my misfortune to discover that my father not only leaves shaving stubble in the sink, but he also leaves the toilet seat up and occasionally unflushed. These are the grisly things a girl is forced to learn when her mother isn't around anymore to cover up.

Dad's waiting for me in the Land Rover that's parked behind the house. Once I get in, he puts the stick shift in reverse, and we back onto the narrow jungle path. Soon we're driving through the center of town. Unlike last night, today we can actually see what's going on here, and it isn't much. A lady with firewood on her head walks past three or four storefronts. The names of the businesses are painted right onto the white concrete buildings. There's THE SLOW BUT SURE SHOP and THE AFRICAN DOCTOR. Above the English words are some words in Chichewa, the other national language in Malawi. The trading center lasts only a minute; then we pass through the jungle again and the shock of where I'm trapped truly sets in.

When a cluster of mud huts with dried-grass roofs appears, Dad pulls off the dirt road. "Here we go!" he says. "Mkumba village." His excitement bounces all over the Land Rover. "So remember, Stallard is the nephew of the chief. I lived in a hut next to his family's."

The afternoon sun is high in the sky, and the shadow of an enormous tree at the edge of the field cuts a sharp line against the ground. I know that if Mom were here, she would make sure I was wearing sunscreen and sunglasses.

I step out of the Land Rover, bare and exposed. The colors are incredibly bright—the yellows, the oranges, even the browns. I can almost picture Mom setting up her easel in the grass. I can almost smell her gluey acrylics as she squeezes them out of the tubes onto her palette. There's a lump growing in my throat, until I catch myself thinking these useless thoughts and tell myself to forget it. Forget her. *Be here now!* I yell in my head. It's what Marcella said I need to do if I don't want to be a miserable human being for the rest of my life.

I take the piece of paper out of the pocket of my dress and hand it to Dad. "What is this?" he asks.

I shrug and he unfolds it. "'Malawi Cultural Manners,'" he reads out loud. "How thoughtful!"

But I'm not thoughtful, just selfish and practical enough to take precautions to avoid complete mortification at any cost. I stare across the field at the people carrying silver buckets on their heads between the huts and the narrow river.

"'Rule Number One,'" Dad reads out loud, "'Don't make contact with elders. Any married person is considered an elder.' Uh-huh. Got that. 'Rule Number Two: If you have guests, don't sweep at night, as it is believed you are chasing them away.'" Dad chuckles. "We don't have to worry about that one!" he says. And it's true. The last time my father picked up a broom was . . . never.

"And finally, 'Rule Number Three: When shaking hands, support the forearm of your greeting hand with the other . . .'"

Suddenly, a bunch of leaves flutter to the ground. I look for a bird or maybe a monkey rustling the branches, but instead I see a flock of little boys. They straddle the limbs of the tree, at least thirty feet above our heads. They point at Dad and me like we're the last living dinosaurs on planet Earth. One boy sits on a branch, his bare foot dipping into the sky like it's a lake. "Hello, *azungu!*" he calls.

Dad smiles and waves. "They're playing tag," he explains, like that's a perfectly normal place to do it. And of course, it's never occurred to me to play tag in the trees, but all of a sudden, I imagine the other possibilities: upside-down tag, tag in the water, tag on the moon.

"*Azungu!*" the boys in the trees shout. I hear a murmur. I look across the field and can't believe what's rushing toward me. I open my mouth and scream, but my scream sounds like a mouse caught in a trap under a dishwasher.

CHAPTER 5

The mob of children arrives. Their sticky fingers poke me, press me. Two tiny girls jump to touch my hair. "Ouch!" I rub my scalp. The girls shriek with laughter and run away, barefoot, across the field. "Dad!" I manage to yell. But he doesn't hear me. He's being attacked too.

Sweat trickles down my forehead as a tall African girl wearing flip-flops elbows her way through the crowd. *"Musiyeni mzanu!"* she yells in a husky voice. She waves her hands and all the barefoot children turn and race back to the village—all except the boys in the trees, and an even smaller boy with a face as round as a full moon. His bright pink bottom lip rolls over in a pout.

"Do not fret," the girl with the husky voice says. "My brother does not desire a turn."

Dad steps closer, puts his arm around my shoulder. I'm so scared that I let him.

"A turn?" I croak.

A tear slides down the boy's dimpled cheek and splashes onto the field grass.

"A turn to touch *azungu*," she says. "White people . . . you."

I point to the tiny boy hiding behind the girl's legs. "Why's he crying?" I ask.

"My brother, Innocent, did only see a few *azungu* in all his life." Her eyes are dark and serious. "He think you are ghost."

"Me, a ghost?" I chuckle. I guess Dad thinks I'm okay, so he takes his arm off my shoulder. But I'm not okay. Not yet. Doesn't he know anything?

Well, I can make people feel better even if my father, the doctor, can't. The boy with the strange name is trembling, so I puff out my cheeks and bang on them. Then I suck the air into my cheeks all over again and curl my index finger, motioning to the boy called Innocent that it's his turn.

Innocent hesitates, but he finally comes close enough for me to take his shaking hands, touch them to my cheeks, and make a noise that sounds exactly like someone who has eaten way too many baked beans. Immediately, his mouth drops open and a giggle flutters out, like a butterfly escaping its cocoon.

"Nice work, Miss Manners," Dad says.

Innocent dashes away, the tall grass swooshing behind him. But I still hear giggles. I look up. The boys in the trees cover their mouths with their hands. Their shoulders shake. One gives me a thumbs-up.

When I look back at Innocent, he is halfway to the

25

huts. He passes a short man in khaki pants and red polo shirt who is running toward Dad and me. "Not again!" I shout to Dad.

"It's Stallard!" Dad tells me. "*Moni*, Stallard!" he calls as I sag with relief.

When we meet, Stallard hugs my father and shakes my hand very formally while holding his own forearm. Then he looks at the girl with the serious eyes. "I see you have met Memory, the daughter of my sister."

"Ahh! Edith's daughter," Dad says, and smiles.

Memory looks shyly at the ground.

"Your mother was a terrific woman," he says.

Memory smiles. But my pulse pounds. *Her mother was a terrific woman? What happened to her mother? Did she die like mine? How did she die? When?*

"So where's Joseph?" Dad asks. "I've got to kick a ball with him."

"The previous hungry season," Stallard says, and sighs. "My brother was weak."

Dad rubs the stubble on his chin. "The . . . ? Oh," he says, and winces. "I'm very sorry to hear that. Very sorry! How is everyone else?"

"Fine, fine." Stallard smiles. "They are most eager to visit with you and your beautiful daughter."

I feel my face turn redder than a theater curtain. Then Stallard and Dad stare in the direction of the huts while I look at this girl named Memory and she looks at me. The hair on my arms stands up and I get a psychic premonition. I know right here and now, way deep inside my bones, that the girl standing beside me is going to become my friend.

26

I've been getting premonitions for as long as I can remember. When my cat Sunny drowned back when I was in third grade, I had a really bad feeling the whole day in school—and that was before I even got home and found out what had happened. And when Mom bought a ticket for the state lottery, she let me pick the numbers. I got one out of four right, and we won five dollars. We would have won five thousand forty-eight dollars, but I put the numbers in the wrong order.

Memory and I follow my father and Stallard toward the drumbeat in the distance, where hundreds of villagers gather, and I quickly lose her in the crowd. "Our new chief," Stallard says. He looks at a thin man with oversized dark glasses and a lavender shirt that says ROCK THE VOTE. I can't believe the chief doesn't wear a headdress. The only cool thing he has is a leather holster tied around his waist. I think there might be a knife in it—probably the knife he uses to defend the village from attack by enemy tribes.

The crowd parts and the new chief reaches us and shakes our hands. Then he claps three times, and men in white robes start to play the most bizarre instruments I've ever seen. One looks like a guitar made from an old gas tank. Two of the men face each other, carrying a pole between them. A drum hangs from the pole. The men bang the drum at the same time while the villagers dance and sing, and the women make high-pitched noises that sound like "la la la la la la la."

When I turn around, I feel a fist right inside me. It's a betrayal of the worst kind: my father's shimmying too. And even though I feel selfish, part of me wants Dad to wait to be happy again. Wait until I'm ready. And I'm not ready. I don't know if I ever will be.

Two village ladies lift my hands and try to dance with me, but I tell them "No thanks." I bite my lip to keep the tears inside. I want the music to stop. I want the dancing to stop.

A few minutes later, my wishes come true. Well, most of them. The music finally stops, and the dancing does too, but my father's still grinning like he's having the time of his life.

A teenage boy leads a goat to the center of the circle. Villagers whoop and howl. The chief pulls out his knife.

I cover my eyes, but I can still hear the goat bleat out its final prayer. Even though the slaughter is over fast, the goat's cries echo in my ears, sending a flurry of shivers up my spine.

Soon a fire rages in the middle of the circle. Flames lick the pastel sky and the smell of cooking meat wafts over me. I am hungry and sickened at the same time. Dad chats with a group of men while the women and girls move to another area.

I slink to the edge of the field. If I could climb the giant tree beside me, I wouldn't play tag. I'd hide in the leaves and never get found.

"Beautiful, the baobab tree," someone says. "Like the African elephant."

I whip my head around.

"My village likes to . . . how do you call . . . ?" Memory purses her lips together and scours the sky. "Party," she says, and smiles. "My village desire to party."

I nod.

28

"Yet you do not appear as if you desire to party," she says. "Perhaps you like to visit my house."

Across the field, I see Dad. I consider telling him that I'm about to disappear. But then again, he was hardly upset last month when I stayed at Marcella's until ten o'clock on a school night, so I figure why bother. It might be good for him to get a little fright.

"*Tiye tonse,*" Memory says. She takes my wrist and leads me away from the clearing. "Home of my family." She points to a hut near the river that looks like all the other huts in Mkumba village. As we walk toward it in the late-afternoon light, field grass whispers across my knees and that word—*family*—lashes my heart like a whip.

CHAPTER 6

It's like someone has taken a hunk of clay and molded an entire village from it. The red dirt rises from the ground to form the hut walls. The roof is covered with dried grass and reeds that droop over the edges. There's no actual door, only a piece of bright orange cloth hanging across the doorway.

Memory kicks off her flip-flops, so I pull off my sandals and leave them beside her shoes on the ground. She pushes the cloth aside, and I follow her in. A second later, I feel like someone's batted a line drive right into my stomach.

The place is half the size of my bedroom in Brookline. How can Memory's whole family fit in here? There isn't any furniture. Not even a bed with an ugly mosquito net. There are a couple of woven mats stretched across the floor, a few pots and spoons huddled in the corner, and some cloths draped over a nail.

And it's snowing.

Well, it's not snowing real snow, of course, but it's snowing the kind of snowflakes you make by folding paper in quarters and cutting out all sorts of geometric designs. These kinds of snowflakes—no two alike—hang from six-inch pieces of yarn all over the ceiling.

I let out my breath. I've escaped the laughter and the music in the field. Maybe Dad's looking for me now. But I'm hidden away here, where it's dark and quiet like a cave.

"The snow is cool," I say.

"Snow?" Memory asks.

I point to the ceiling.

"Ahhh . . . yes, very cold." She wraps her arms around her chest and pretends to shiver.

"I mean it's cool, as in I really like it," I say.

"*Zikomo*," Memory says. "I made it in the school the year we own sufficient paper. Are you hungry? Perhaps you desire *nsima?*"

"Is it goat?" My voice is groggy, weak. I've barely used it in days.

Memory laughs. "*Nsima* is not goat. It is grain. The goat shall take hours to cook."

"Grain I can deal with," I say.

"*Nsima* made from maize. I think you shall like. I hope you shall like, as here in Malawi, we eat *nsima* morning, noon, and night. In the case you do not like our *nsima*, you have troubles," she says, and laughs. "Large troubles."

Memory pushes aside a piece of cloth at the other end of the hut. Behind it is a tiny sort of closet. On the floor of the closet is a small pile of corncobs that look like they've been there forever, because the kernels are withered and dried. "The hungry season will end soon," she says as she lifts the edge of her skirt and places eight cobs inside. "The harvest will come and our maize silo will be full again." She carries the corncobs over to a clay bowl and drops them in.

"Can I help you?" I ask.

"A visitor for one minute shall hold the hoe in two minutes' time," she says, and hands me the bowl full of corncobs that's much heavier than it looks. When I take it, my bicep throbs where I got all those shots for the trip.

I rub my arm while Memory rolls open a mat on the dried-mud floor. I plop down on it. She squats beside me and shows me how to tear off the kernels. Our fingers look strange beside each other's. Hers are callused and rough, used to the job. I still have specks of red nail polish on mine.

"You do this," Memory says. "I make the *ndiwo*." She stands and walks two steps back to the hidden closet and pulls out an onion. She carries it to the mat with a knife and chops the onion into another bowl. "You will like *ndiwo*. You will see." Memory presses the sleeve of her dress into the corner of her tearing eyes.

"I hope I can learn Chichewa half as *bwino* as your English," I say, and squint. My eyes are burning from the onion too. But thanks to Marcella, I know how to solve this problem. Since kindergarten, Marcella's taught me plenty of tricks. How to get rid of hiccups? Stand on your head and drink water from a straw. How to pop a zit? Steam your face over a pot of boiling water first. And how to cut an onion without feeling like your eyeballs are on fire?

"I've got just the thing," I say. I reach into my knapsack and pull out a pack of Juicy Fruit gum that's left over from the flight. "Here." I hand Memory a piece. "It's a trick. Chew."

She unwraps the gum from the silver foil.

"Mmmm!" She smiles and pops it into her mouth. We both chew our gum, and our eyes don't tear up anymore. "This magic gum from America work real good," she says, and we go back to work.

Once I've got all the kernels in the bowl, Memory uses a rock to grind them into a fine powder that looks like flour. She cuts up a tomato and some greens. Then she gathers supplies from the dark corner of the hut and tells me to follow her outside. Of course, I don't want to go. It feels good inside the small, damp hut, but I can't say that I'm staying put. I'm a guest, after all. And even though I've had a premonition, we're not friends *yet*.

So I leave the hut through the curtain. While Memory lights her own fire, I watch the villagers across the field still celebrating our arrival. They are dancing and eating and singing, so happy that my father is back in the neighborhood.

Memory sets a pot on top of three stones, sticks the firewood underneath, and strikes a match. Once the fire's lit, she picks up a bottle and pours the yellow Kazinga oil into the pot and fries the onion until it sizzles.

Something about that sizzling sound makes me realize that my bladder's about to explode. I touch my tongue to the top of my mouth, roll my eyes to the sky, and bite the inside of my cheek. But this time Marcella's trick doesn't work. I still have to go to the bathroom. And I guess crossing your legs is an international sign for "When you've gotta go, you've gotta go," because Memory points to a small hut nearby and says, "The ladies' is there." So I buckle on my sandals and bolt across the dirt to a hut that actually has a door made of bamboo poles. I pinch my nose and push it open.

Inside, it's completely dark except for a narrow rectangle of light at the top of the wall. My eyeballs reach, reach, reach for the light, and the light reach, reach, reaches for my eyeballs, and when the two finally connect, I figure out there isn't a toilet in sight.

I pace in a little circle, trying to figure out what to do. My foot slams into something hard. Some kind of lid. I trace a metal square with my toe. I bend down and thread my finger through a loop on the top of the lid and try to heave it aside. It's so heavy, though, I need two hands. Even though I quickly hold my nose again, it's too late— the odor quivers inside my nostrils like a sour mist. But at least I think I understand how this "bathroom" works. Finally, I get down to business. And for a split second, I'm not worried about the dark, or the snakes, or the smell.

I just stare at the flies buzzing in the wave of dusty light shining through the window slit. When I'm through, I squint around for some toilet paper. My eyes have adjusted to the light and I can see a bit. But unfortunately, although I do have a keen psychic ability, I cannot conjure objects from thin air, and I especially cannot create toilet paper when there isn't any.

CHAPTER 7

"Hold your hands here," Memory says when I return from the bathroom. She pours water from the bucket for me. "My turn," she says, and I pour the water for her. Then we're ready to eat. I take off my sandals and help carry the food back inside the hut, where we sit on the mats.

Memory tears off a hunk of *nsima*, rolls the dough into a ball in her fingers, and dips it in the *ndiwo*. "Do like this," she says, and takes a bite. "The good report is you only miss five days of term two at Mzanga Full Primary School." But then I realize that Memory's good report comes with a bad report: We aren't going to be setting down any plates or forks or knives or spoons. We'll be eating with our hands. "Uncle Stallard explains you shall be in my class, standard eight. My brother Innocent attend this school also. He attend standard one."

Even though most Global Health Project doctors who come to Malawi from the United States send their kids to the boarding school in Blantyre, Dad wants me to go to the local school. He says that way I'll get the real village experience. "Besides," he told me, "I want to spend more family time together." Since when is two people enough for a family? At least Memory has a father plus a brother, so that makes a more normal number: three. Maybe she knows how long the pain lasts. Maybe she can tell me when I'll stop waking up with tears on my pillow. But how can I ask her when we've only just met?

I rip off a small piece of *nsima*. I roll it in my hands and sniff. Surprise, surprise. It smells like corn.

"Do not worry," Memory says. "This food I cook is not bewitched."

"Oh, I, uh . . . I was about to dig in!" I sink the little piece of dough into the *ndiwo* and shove it into my mouth.

"In our class at Mzanga Full Primary is best students in villages," Memory says. "Agnes is number two student. She bony and how do you say . . . *satana?*" Memory can't think of how to say the word in English, so we move on to the other students: Saidi, Norman, and Patuma. "The girl called Patuma fancy the boy called Norman," she says, before discussing the other girls: Stella, Winnie, and Sickness.

"Sickness? This is someone's name?" I ask.

"Not a good name," says Memory. "She supposed to die when she born, but she live. Her mum give her this name."

"Oh," I say, and take another bite of *nsima* with *ndiwo*.

It's getting darker in the hut, and I don't see lamps or

lightbulbs anywhere. "Do you have uniform prepared?" Memory asks.

I shake my head. "What uniform?"

She stands. *"Tiye tonse,"* she says. Even though that phrase wasn't on the vocabulary list I studied before I left, I'm getting the feeling it means something like "Follow the leader" or "Better get a move on."

Outside, Memory shows me a dress that's hanging from a clothesline behind the hut. In the dusk, I can't tell if it's blue or green or gray, but I can see the shape of it just fine. I don't mean to be rude, but it looks like a pilgrim frock. Still, I'm a firm believer in stretching the truth in the name of friendship. At this rate, Memory might be the only person I'm speaking to on the entire African continent, so I tell her "It's sooo cool!" even though I'd never be caught dead wearing something like that myself.

"Do not worry," she says. "The village seamstress shall fix you a uniform in two days. Now let us fetch your daddy."

I put on my sandals and follow her across the field. Halfway back to the party, I stop in the moonlit grass to watch the silhouette of a grasshopper. The grasshopper wobbles across the dirt like an old African queen, until she remembers that she's still young and jumps up as high as my eyeballs. I gasp and Memory just laughs as we trudge the rest of the way to the clearing.

I'm sure Dad is panicked by now. I mean, it's dark and I'm missing and I could've been attacked by a wild beast. There are leopards and lions and zebras in this part of Malawi. Suddenly, I feel a little guilty. He was probably so worried that he sent out a search party to find me. I run to the smoldering fire, where he's sitting with Stallard, the new chief, and another man. They're all perched in carved wooden chairs, watching the poor goat cook.

I walk between Dad and the fire. Memory shuffles up behind me. At first, Dad doesn't notice I'm there, so I pace back and forth a few times until he calls out, "Hey, Clare!"

I whip my head toward him, even though I don't really mean to. And in the flickering firelight, I see my father grinning like he doesn't have a care in the world. "Honey," he says, "I'd like you to meet Bright Malola. Mr. Malola is the clinical officer at the hospital where I'll be working. Bright, this is my beautiful daughter, Clare."

I blush while the gap-toothed man beside my father stands and smiles. I quickly remember not to make eye contact because it's considered rude. So I look off to the spit while my skin throbs in the muggy night. I blink a few times and grind my teeth into my pendant. But talk about rude! My own father didn't even notice I was gone.

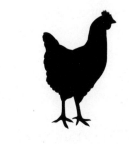

CHAPTER 8

D read.
　　I dread waking up more than I can say. And so I try my best not to.

For the third time, Dad reaches his hand under the net and gives me a little shove. "Rise and shine," he says again.

I pull the pillow over my head.

He's sniffing something. "Wow, Clare," he says. "You still smell smoky." He's smelling me!

I groan.

"What did Memory cook for you over at her place?"

My eyes fling open. How did he know where I was last night? I consider breaking my no-talking policy to ask, but I don't get a chance, because the strangest thing happens: a deep, throaty laugh rumbles through my bedroom like an earthquake.

The laugh throws me into a state of shock and panic. No way am I in the mood for a visitor!

"Put on your clothes and I'll introduce you," Dad says. I roll over.

"Might I remind you," he says, "this is going to be a very long trip if you're planning not to talk to me."

Dad pulls the mosquito netting aside. Before I set my feet on the floor, I close my eyes and offer up a quick but heartfelt prayer: *God, if you exist, please make Memory want to sit next to me in the cafeteria at my new school today. I beg of you!* Then I stretch my arms over my head and yawn.

"So, guess," Dad says. He's trying to trick me into talking to him, but I'm not falling for it. Diamond-shaped shadows from the mosquito net dance on the walls. I trace their pattern with my eyes.

"C'mon, guess!"

Huge ants swarm the crumpled-up mini Hershey Bar wrapper I left on the dresser last night. No doubt they stumbled on the treasure in the bloodshot hours of the night and carried each other piggyback to the site, the entire procession hypnotized by the sweet scent. There isn't anything left on the foil wrapper, but still, the ants massacre it with glee.

Dad clasps his hands behind his back and rocks on his toes. I can see he's dying to tell me. Even though I don't ask, he can't stand the suspense. "The new maid!" he says. "This place comes with a maid. I didn't even know it. It said so in the paperwork but somehow I missed it."

I pretend I'm searching for something in the dresser, but really what I'm doing is thinking. I'm thinking that most kids would probably be completely stoked to have someone cook and clean for them, someone who's around to take care of the house. Not me. That's because I know better. I know you need a mother to make a house a home. No one else can do it, no matter how hard they try.

"Get dressed and come meet Mrs. Bwanali," Dad says, and leaves.

I run to the bathroom and turn the faucet knob, and, lucky me, five trickles of freezing cold water spurt out of the rusty showerhead. While my hair gets wet, I think about all the people who tried to rush in to fill the empty spots during the past eight months since my mother died.

In the beginning, Mom's friends came over with casseroles and lasagnas and meat loaves. They tidied up the kitchen while their kids watched TV or hung out in the playroom and tried their best to act like everything was practically normal, like I was still the same. But we all knew the truth: overnight, I had become a freak. I mean, there were plenty of kids walking around with divorced parents, but only a handful with dead ones. Grandma came from Sacramento for the whole month of August, and that was a little better. She took me shopping on Newbury Street and we baked lace cookies together. Of course, I totally love Grandma and everything, but in the end, she couldn't replace my mother either.

Dad bangs on the bathroom door. "There's no time for a shower this morning, Clare," he yells. But he must be kidding! Does he really think I'd go to school smelling like smoke? I furiously rub the shampoo into my hair.

"Come on, kiddo. You need to get out right now," he says.

I partially rinse out the shampoo and open the yellow

bottle of something called *après-shampooing lissant*. I took it from the Paris hotel where we stayed last year when Dad had a pediatric surgery conference. I'm working the *après-shampooing lissant* through from the roots to the ends when Dad pounds on the door again. "Not only are we running late, Clare, but you're probably using up our water supply for the next month!"

Okay, that's a terrifying thought! Even though my hair is still coated with *lissant*, I get out. I'll just hope the potion left on my head evaporates with the water as my hair dries.

Back in the bedroom, I pull on my magenta cotton V-neck tee, brown crinkled bedouin skirt, and earth-tone beaded earrings. It's a million degrees here and women aren't supposed to wear shorts. How messed up is that? I use my experience creating costumes for the school plays to make myself look respectable. I pin my hair back with four retro poodle barrettes I bought for the Pink Ladies in *Grease*, and when there are no obvious fixes left, I go into the kitchen to meet our new maid, otherwise known as the intruder.

CHAPTER 9

Mrs. Bwanali is an enormous woman wrapped in a purple, yellow, and green floral-print skirt and a red paisley shirt. I squint to protect my eyes from the clashing patterns and colors. She's sitting at the kitchen table with my father, a plate of orange squashy stuff between them. The only thing that looks worse than her fashion sense is her cooking. As far as I'm concerned, she can leave right now.

"Ahh . . . Clare!" she says. She smiles and the fat on her cheeks swallows her eyes. "It is a pleasure to meet you." She stands and grabs my hands with hers. "A true and most superior pleasure."

Dad is so excited about her that he forgets to chew me out about the shower. In fact, he's acting rather civilized. "Clare, did you know that Mrs. Bwanali lives in Kapoloma village?" he says. "She's worked at this house for sixteen years. She and her husband are originally from Zambia."

"We are from Tanzania, then Zambia," Mrs. Bwanali says.

But I have no idea where either of those places is. And does it really matter? This woman won't be here long. I won't let her.

"You are a precious girl," Mrs. Bwanali tells me. "I do hope you enjoy boiled pumpkin. Dr. Heath looooved boiled pumpkin."

Dad told me that Dr. Heath is the woman who lived in this house before us. She also worked for the Global Health Project. When she returned to England, she left a pair of gold hoop earrings on the living room table and a red umbrella next to the front door.

"I cook treats for Dr. Heath and I cook treats for you," Mrs. Bwanali says. "You need good food, good story, Mrs. Bwanali is here."

She sets a plate and a fork down in front of me. I stab the fork into a slice and flop it onto my plate. When I shove a small piece into my mouth, a shocking burst of sweetness cascades over my tongue. Before I can stop myself, I make a huge mistake by uttering one itty-bitty three-letter word: "Yum!"

"Yum?" Mrs. Bwanali leans over me. "Is this good?"

"Very good," Dad says.

The damage has been done. Mrs. Bwanali stands up straight and grins until her eyes disappear into the folds on her face again. "A real Malawi girl, Clare. You and me, we are friends."

Suddenly, my stomach is in more knots than my macramé handbag—the one in my closet back in Brookline.

"Do I need to bring a lunch to school?" I ask. I doubt I'll be in the mood to eat later, but better safe than sorry.

"It is not necessary," Mrs. Bwanali says. "This is the purpose of the big-size breakfast." She turns on the faucet and sings as she rinses a pot.

"I don't think you'll need to pay," Dad says. "I think they've got porridge for free. But take this just in case." He opens his wallet and hands me a hundred *kwacha*. "It's about sixty-five cents," Dad whispers. I guess he doesn't want Mrs. Bwanali to hear him talking about money. Maybe it would make her feel bad. I'm not really sure. "Should be plenty," he says, and of course, I take it because I don't have any Malawian money of my own.

When Mrs. Bwanali finishes washing the pot, she turns to me and says, "Miss Clare, do you enjoy the egg fried or mixed or with the sunshine side up?"

"No thanks," I tell her, and pop another little piece of pumpkin into my mouth. "No egg for me."

"You are a growing girl. It is a long day at the school. I must suggest you eat."

I've had enough. I stand to head back to my room, but Mrs. Bwanali wedges herself in the doorway between the kitchen and living room. There's no way around her.

"Yoo-hoo!" she calls, waving her hand to get my attention, never mind that I'm only one foot away. "Yoo-hoo, Clare!" she says again. She throws her head back and laughs. "I do like this word, *yoo-hoo*. Dr. Heath teach me

45

this word. I have something for you. Stop there." She takes two steps away from me, turns again. "No moving your muscle!"

I hold my hands up and freeze while she disappears through the kitchen to the veranda. A second later, Mrs. Bwanali's standing in front of me, proudly holding a school uniform like the one Memory showed me last night. Except the bad news is that I can see it better in daylight, and it's even uglier than I thought. Plus, it's aquamarine blue.

"For you!" she says, and beams. "A gift from the fourthborn daughter of my sister Betty. This girl graduated Mzanga Full Primary last year. She is called Sakina. She said it her large honor to give you this dress."

Not only is Sakina's honor large, but her dress is too. It looks about six sizes too big for me, and it has at least four holes around the hem.

"I . . . I don't know what to say," I tell Mrs. Bwanali.

Dad's eyebrows fly up and down, up and down superfast. I get the text. "Thank you," I mutter.

"You must hurry," Mrs. Bwanali says. "Put it on. You shall look like every schoolgirl then, ready to learn your lessons."

"Hurry up and change," Dad says.

I bug out my eyes in protest.

"Now!" he growls.

So I take the dress from Mrs. Bwanali and run to my bedroom, where I throw off my awesome outfit, pull on the atrocious dress, and glimpse at thirty-six square inches of me at a time in the bathroom mirror. Then I sit on my bed under the netting and burst into tears.

"Come, Miss Clare," Mrs. Bwanali calls from the kitchen. "Let us have a look-see, shall we?"

I wipe the tears on the back of my hand, blow my nose in the bathroom, and trudge back in there. As soon as she sees me, Mrs. Bwanali claps her hands together and says, "You are real Malawi schoolgirl. Gorgeous like a guinea fowl!"

My jaw drops. A *guinea fowl!*

Dad hands me a bottle of water and a tube of sunscreen. "Put it on in the car," he says. He lifts the strap of his briefcase over his shoulder, and I follow him outside.

While we back out of the driveway in the Land Rover, Mrs. Bwanali stands in the doorway and shouts "Toodle-oo!" at the top of her lungs. She would wake the whole neighborhood, if only we had one.

CHAPTER 10

Dad pulls onto a patch of dirt at the top of a hill. Below us, a bunch of long, skinny buildings with tin roofs stretch across the dirt like silver vipers. I'd be excited to leave this Land Rover, to escape from my father, except that now we're at my new school. Dad gets out, walks around, and opens the door on my side. "Honey," he says. "I know you're scared, but I want you to trust me." I look away, down the hill at the school. A chill runs through me. "I love you very much," he says. "Your mother would be proud."

I grab my backpack off the seat and step out. Then I walk behind my father, who lopes down the hill in his plastic clogs like a marionette whose puppeteer is busy scratching an itch with the other hand. If I was speaking to Dad, I would tell him that it may be my first day of school in a new country in the middle of nowhere, but that doesn't mean I need him. I can make my grand entrance alone. But since I can't talk and there's no way to communicate such an important message through body language, I let Dad accompany me all the way there, like I'm a kid going to her first day of kindergarten.

We're a few yards away from a small brick structure set off from the other buildings when a short man in a three-piece suit limps out of the door. A bead of sweat inches down the side of my face. I twist my hair into a short ponytail and let the air dry my neck.

"Welcome to Mzanga Full Primary!" the man calls out, and smiles. He pulls a red handkerchief out of his pocket. "Pardon," he says, and pats it against the glistening skin of his forehead. "We are most pleased with your arrival. I am the headmaster, Mr. Kingsley." He turns to Dad. "You may refer to me by my given name, Special."

"Thank you, Special," my father says without even cracking a smile.

No sooner has Mr. Special Kingsley shaken hands with us than a husky voice calls out, "Hello!"

I peek around Dad and Mr. Special Kingsley, only to discover Memory standing in the doorway of the headmaster's office. She's waiting for me. "*Moni*," I say, using one of the words from the vocabulary list I studied.

"Memory tells me you visited with her in the village last night," the headmaster says. "I asked her to greet you and escort you to class this morning."

Dad checks his watch yet again. "We're very sorry we're late," he says.

Mr. Special Kingsley looks at me. "School begins at seven-thirty a.m. unless there are quizzes. Then six-thirty

49

a.m. Shall we say we will excuse it on this, your very first day at Mzanga? However, Clare, let us not make it a habit."

"No," I say. "No habit. No, sir."

Mr. Special Kingsley chuckles and follows a rooster with frayed feathers into his office. The rooster pecks at our feet while Mr. Special Kingsley removes a black notebook from the drawer of a beaten-up wooden desk and asks Dad to sign me in on the school register. As Dad completes the information, I explain to Memory about Mrs. Bwanali's sister Betty's fourth-born daughter, Sakina, who gave me the uniform.

"Fantastic!" she says.

After Dad writes our name and address in the notebook, he actually rubs my head. "Pick you up after school," he says. Then he shakes my new headmaster's hand, completely forgetting to hold his forearm.

"I shall watch your daughter with care and kind wishes," Mr. Special Kingsley says. After Dad leaves the office, my headmaster turns to me. "I would like you to know, Clare, that your friend Memory is a most shining scholar."

But I don't care if she's smart, dumb, serious, or funny. I'm just happy she's here.

"This girl also tends to the books for the entire school," Mr. Special Kingsley says. "Each day, she carries all fifty-three books five kilometers to the village for safe-keeping from rains and thieves."

Memory stares at the floor. "It is nothing, sir," she says.

But it is not nothing. It is something. It is something that she is standing beside me, the new girl, without caring what the other kids might say. It is something that she helped me survive the night and cooked me grain instead of goat, when she probably would have had fun at the village celebration with her other friends.

"Memory shall take you to class now," my new headmaster says.

And even though being here with Memory is something, it is not enough. Not enough for me to want to stay at this school for another minute, let alone a whole day. I want to go back to Brookline, where I belong. Back to Brookline, where my best friend has known me since kindergarten, not less than twenty-four hours. Back to Brookline, where the principal's office doesn't have roosters prancing inside it.

But things only go from bad to worse, because as Memory leads me alongside the mud-brick school building, I make the unfortunate mistake of looking into one of the classrooms. It's not like I expect to see recessed lighting and swivel chairs with a SMART Board. That said, what on earth can prepare a girl like me to see birds' nests in the classroom ceilings?

"This is where my brother learns," she says. "Standard one."

"Standard one?" I croak. "Is that first grade?"

"The infant class. *Inde*, you can call this the first grade."

I can only see a bit into the classroom. The teacher, a pregnant woman with a high head of hair, stands up front. The children are crowded together on the floor. All the girls have on the same sorry dress I do, and the boys wear khaki shorts and short-sleeved aquamarine button-down shirts. Their skinny legs stick out straight in front of them.

Now Memory speaks and walks faster. She's heading

51

for a classroom at the very end of the school building. "I shall now tell you again of the standard eight students. Saidi, bright spirit. Nice to see." She smiles. "Winnie, small and surprising." She takes a breath. "Most significant information is this: Agnes. Do you remember what I tell you about Agnes?"

I shake my head no.

"She is not satisfactory. She is number two student. Bony girl, and very, very *satana*."

It hits me right then that the word *satana* sounds an awful lot like Satan.

"Ancestors curse me. I share table with this girl," she says. "Our teacher request for you to sit between Agnes and me." We reach the doorway. But I'd rather get my braces back on and eat taffy than go in there.

CHAPTER 11

For a second, I'm relieved to see that there aren't a million kids stuck all over the floor like pins crammed into a pincushion. Instead, there are about twenty students crowded onto wooden benches behind rectangular tables. The teacher is standing at the front of the room in a white, yellow, and gold dress. She looks like a piece of popcorn. When she sees me, she closes the book in her hands and lays it on the metal table. "Glorious! Glorious!" she says, and everyone in the entire room turns to stare.

All of a sudden, my whole body freezes. I'm not making up some sort of dramatic, hyperbole type of thing. What I'm saying is a serious fact: my heart actually stops beating, and my blood completely stops pumping, and my lungs totally stop breathing. I know, because as hard as I try to take a step, I can't. Meanwhile, Memory holds out her hand like she's the hostess at Zaftigs Delicatessen showing me to a seat. I know it's Agnes sitting on the bench there, because she's bony, like a lamb chop after someone's eaten off all the meat.

After a couple of seconds, Memory grabs my wrist and yanks me forward. Somehow the spell is broken. I take out my notebook and purple feather pen, and I wiggle onto the bench beside Agnes. Then Memory shoves in next to me, so I'm the egg salad between two pieces of dark rye in a very squishy sandwich. There isn't even enough room between us to slip in one sheet of lettuce or a thin slice of tomato.

"I am Mrs. Tomasi," the teacher says, and smiles. "And you . . ." She tilts her head slowly. "You are a blessing. A glorious blessing from America." She puts her hands together in front of her chest in a prayer position, cocks her head to the side, and smiles.

"Thanks," I mumble. Trust me, I'd much rather be invisible than a blessing. But I guess after that introduction, Agnes figures she'll get another look at me. She turns her head for a quick second, and when she does, her lamb chop elbow pokes into my rib cage.

"Here in Malawi, we are fortunate to speak many languages," Mrs. Tomasi says. "In fact, class, let us tell Clare our school rules." Benches scrape against the floor. Everyone stands. Since I'm part of the Memory-Agnes sandwich, I have no choice but to stand up too while the kids recite this poem:

"We work hard,
Respect our elders,
Also we have one more rule:

Here at Mzanga Full Primary,
We speak English while at school."

"You may be seated, class," Mrs. Tomasi says, and the Memory-Agnes sandwich falls back onto our bench. "You see, Clare, Mr. Kingsley believes all the students shall do well to practice English. Our youngest students shall learn the English alphabet this year. Most of our students do speak Chichewa at home, as well as a third tribal language. What languages do you speak, Clare?"

Before Mom died, I was on the honor roll for three years in a row. The last thing I need is to be grilled on my academic achievement. "I speak English," I squeak out.

Everyone giggles.

Okay, I guess that's pretty obvious, but I'm not finished. "And Spanish," I add. Why not? I already know my Spanish numbers, the colors, and the alphabet, and I can conjugate a bunch of verbs. So what if I can't exactly speak a Spanish sentence yet? I seriously don't see any reason why it shouldn't count.

"Lovely," Mrs. Tomasi says, her voice smooth as melted butter. "Boys and girls, we shall make an exception to the rule for our American student. We shall teach her Chichewa during her visit to Malawi. Then she shall speak three languages as all of you do.

"Boys and girls, what words does Clare need to know?" Mrs. Tomasi asks the class.

"*Muli bwanji,*" says a tall boy who sits in the front of the classroom.

I already know that *muli bwanji* means "How are you?" All of the most basic phrases were on the list Dad gave

55

me. Still, I keep my mouth shut because I don't want to act like a smart aleck.

"Norman, tell our new friend what *muli bwanji* means," Mrs. Tomasi says.

The boy turns in his seat. His dark eyes sparkle. "'How do you?'" he says.

"'How *are* you?'" Mrs. Tomasi corrects. "Your turn, Clare. *Muli bwanji?* How are you?"

"Thirsty," I croak. "I'm a little thirsty."

Holy mackerel! You'd think I said *My rear end is sunburned.* Everyone chokes out these quiet little laughs, Memory and Agnes included, which means that my rib cage gets poked from both sides this time.

"Clare," Mrs. Tomasi says, "you shall say what I do. *Muli bwanji?*"

A light goes on in my brain: a flashing red doofus light! I'm not supposed to *answer* the question, only repeat it. I reach to the floor for my bag, but we're packed in so tight that Memory has to get up in order for me to grab hold of it. I pull my water bottle out and suck half of it down, not only because I'm thirsty, but also because I need to extinguish the fire that's burning up my face. While I guzzle, Agnes and Memory both stare. I get the distinct feeling I should offer them some water, but my dentist told me kids can get gum disease from sharing drinks, so, really fast, I twist the cap back on and chuck the bottle into my bag.

When we finally get past the whole *muli bwanji* situation, Mrs. Tomasi asks, "What other words shall we teach Clare?"

The boy who sits at the table in front of me raises his

56

hand. His hand has a scar the shape of Florida on it. When Mrs. Tomasi calls on him, he turns and looks at me. "*Chabwino*," he says. "It mean 'wonderful.'"

"Your turn, Clare," Mrs. Tomasi says.

I can hardly get air into my lungs to activate my vocal cords, but somehow, I manage that one little word: "*Chabwino*."

When Mrs. Tomasi asks for yet another vocabulary suggestion, Agnes's hand shoots up.

"Yes, Agnes?" our teacher says.

Agnes's voice is sharp like her bones. "*Bongololo*," she says.

"Why must our new student know *bongololo*?" Mrs. Tomasi asks.

Agnes leans over the side of her desk, and as she reaches for something on the floor, she pokes me with her elbow for a third time. When she sits back up, she dangles a hideous hairy wormy creature in front of me. My heart hammers in my chest.

"Agnes," Mrs. Tomasi shouts, "this is not how we treat visitors!"

Agnes finally moves the snake away from my face.

Mrs. Tomasi sighs. "In English, you call this centipede. In Chichewa, we say *bongololo*."

I take another look. That's when I see it's true. The little thing does have a hundred squirmy legs that are all wiggling in different directions at the exact same time. "*Bongololo*," I whisper while Mrs. Tomasi points to the doorway and Agnes flings the vile bug outside.

"What do I tell you?" Memory says, loud enough for Agnes to hear. "The girl is *satana*."

I nod once. Then I crack the knuckles on each of my fingers and pray, pray, pray that I won't cry.

After vocabulary, it's time for math. "Handlebar," Mrs. Tomasi says, "please fetch a new chalk."

"Handlebar?" I whisper to Memory.

"Before the birth of this boy, the father ride the mother to hospital to deliver baby," Memory whispers. "The mother sit on bicycle handlebar to get there."

I never thought about it before, but suddenly, I want to know what my mother was doing right before I was born. Watching a movie on the couch? Walking through a museum? Was she nauseous? Did she feel fine? What did she do when she felt me kick really hard? Was she scared or excited? And did she ever consider naming me anything but Clare? I feel like a book with the pages torn out at the best part.

When Handlebar returns to the classroom a few minutes later, he's holding something that looks like a potato. With a small knife, Mrs. Tomasi peels off the top of the vegetable and uses it to write equations on the board, until finally, Mr. Special Kingsley rings his bell. Must be time for lunch. "Excuse me," I say to Memory. "I need to get my bag."

"Oh, no!" Memory tells me. "It is not the time you think." Agnes cackles and Mrs. Tomasi says, "Mr. Kingsley rings bell to send youngest students home. The senior classes learn for many more hours."

"Well, then, when do we eat lunch?" I whisper to Memory. But it's Agnes who answers.

"My profound and sincere apology to the Glorious Blessing from America," she says. "Here in the Warm Heart of Africa, we do not eat lunch."

Tears burn the corners of my eyes. I try Marcella's trick: I press my tongue against the roof of my mouth and silently recite the alphabet backward. My tears stay hidden, but my stomach growls right out loud.

"Perhaps if you drink the rest of your store-bought water," Agnes says, "your American belly shall feel full."

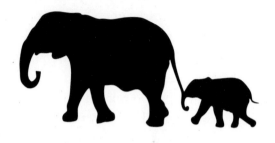

CHAPTER 12

By the time school really lets out, I don't even know if I have enough energy to walk up the hill. Dad's surrounded by kids. They check out the Land Rover like it's a rocket ship while he presses his stethoscope onto one little chest after the next.

When I show up, he pats the top of my head. *"Muli bwanji?"* he asks, as if the silent treatment is so old I'll probably just forget about it. I throw open the Land Rover door and get in. While I wait for him, I decide he's right. This silent treatment is getting tired, so as soon as he wraps the stethoscope around his neck and opens the door, I scream, "Hungry! For your information, they don't even serve lunch in this place!"

Dad looks surprised, but I don't know if he's surprised because I've actually spoken or surprised about lunch.

I fold my arms and stare out the window.

"I thought they'd at least give you some porridge," he says. "That's what they always used to do." He turns the key and waits for the swarm of kids to get out of the way.

"I want to get out of here," I say.

Dad reaches over and takes my hand. I pull it away. As soon as we turn into the driveway, I throw open the Land Rover door and run right past Mrs. Bwanali, who's carrying a bucket of clothes outside to wash by hand. It looks like it's going to take her forever. Too bad this dumb house doesn't come with a washing machine.

I slam my bedroom door shut and yank off my sneakers. They are teeming with heat. I also tear off my soggy socks and shove on the ruby slippers Marcella wore when she played Dorothy last year. She gave them to me as a going-away present. "Just so you'll remember there's no place like home," she'd said.

I climb under the mosquito net and collapse in bed on my stomach. A minute later, Dad knocks on the door. I don't say anything, but he goes ahead and trespasses because there isn't even a lock on the door.

"Where'd you get those?" he asks.

I bang my heels together three times. One of the slippers falls off and clatters to the floor.

"Here," he says. He pushes aside the mosquito net and throws a banana and a bag of chips onto my bed. The bag crackles as I pull it open and inhale the salty potato scent.

"I've got to get back to the hospital for a few hours. But, Clare?"

I chomp on a pile of chips.

"You're going to be fine."

Then that's it. Dad walks out of the room and out of the house. Lately, I wish he'd walk out of my life.

I'm sketching a self-portrait. I'm lost on a raft in the ocean. I doubt anyone will ever find me. There's a shark fin in the background. Maybe I'll get eaten. Or maybe first I'll starve.

Mrs. Bwanali knocks on the door. "Yoo-hoo!" she calls.

"Come in," I mutter.

She carries over a tray with *nsima* and boiled pumpkin. "For you," she says. But other than those two words, she doesn't try to talk to me at all. She doesn't pull aside the net and sneak a peek at my sketchpad either. She just sets down the tray on top of the dresser, and before I can say *zikomo*, she's gone.

So I eat in my bed while I watch the sky change colors out the window—dianthus pink, manganese blue, cobalt violet. It's shortly after I hear the first bush baby cry that I remember the night critters, and I carry the empty tray back into the kitchen, where Mrs. Bwanali's standing at the stove. Lentils whimper at the bottom of her pot under a cloud of smoke.

She stirs the beans. "Mrs. Bwanali can talk," she says. "Yes, but Mrs. Bwanali do listen even more good. You know, Clare, I have five daughters of my own. These ears listen better than a dog."

I think about it then. Here she is, cooking for Dad and me, cleaning our house. Who is cooking and cleaning for her family? I wonder what daydreams whisper to her while her pot sizzles, what pictures glitter in her mind.

"It was yummy," I say. I set the tray on the counter and leave to go back to my room.

"Clare, before you exit, I must tell you what we say here in Malawi."

I turn in the doorway between the kitchen and the living room.

"We say *mwana wa m'zako ndiwako yemwe*." She tosses the dishrag over her shoulder and walks toward me. "What does this mean?" she asks, and takes my hands in hers. "It mean 'the child that belong to my neighbor also belong to me.'"

I swallow. I want to stay in the kitchen with Mrs. Bwanali, but even though she likes to listen, I don't know what I'd say. I mean, how do you explain to someone that a part of you has died? How do you tell someone that you feel like a ghost without a soul?

You don't.

Which is why I mutter "Bye" to Mrs. Bwanali. Then I wander back to my bedroom, stretch out on my bed, and fade into the indigo night.

CHAPTER 13

Dad shakes me awake. "Feeling better?"

For a second I am, until I blink a few times and realize that it's already the next morning. I fell asleep in my uniform, and now it's a wrinkled mess.

"Good news," Dad says. I can't imagine what it could be. "While you were sleeping, I tightened the pipes. Shower's working better. But keep it short or we're going to run out by the end of the day."

I walk to the bathroom and turn the shower on. Lo and behold, it is good news. Now there are eight strands of water coming out instead of five. I scrub myself with a washcloth, but even with the increased water pressure, no matter how hard I rub my skin, I'm covered with dirt. It's under my fingernails, in the cracks between my toes. I haven't even put the shampoo in my hair when the showerhead sputters and half the water strands disappear. At this rate, I'll run out of water with a headful of soapsuds. I cut my losses and get out.

I put on my rumpled uniform again, since I have to wear the same thing to school every day except for Wednesday, uniform wash day. When I tromp into the kitchen, Mrs. Bwanali says, "Do this dress wrinkle in the sun like a dried fish?"

"I slept in it," I say, embarrassed that I didn't even have the energy to change out of my clothes last night.

Mrs. Bwanali sets breakfast on the table—boiled cassava, avocado, and eggs. As I swallow it down like a python swallowing a pig, Mrs. Bwanali says, "I shall find some hot rocks."

"Hot rocks?"

"To press the uniform," she says.

Dad stands in the kitchen doorway and checks his watch. "I'm afraid we don't have time for ironing right now," he says. "Today Clare's going to get to school on time."

I bug out my eyes and silently plead with Mrs. Bwanali for help.

"The hot rock special iron do not take long, Dr. Silver," she says. "I fear that I cannot let this beautiful girl attend school in a dried fish uniform. You shall sit and drink Mrs. Bwanali's sugared tea and read your report and get smart. It shall take only a minute."

"But—" Dad begins.

"But you shall sit like a king in his throne," Mrs. Bwanali says, pulling out the kitchen chair. She waits for

Dad to sit before she takes the pot off the stove and pours him a cup of tea.

As I traipse down the hill to school in my perfectly ironed uniform, I scour the field for anyone who looks familiar. There are hundreds of students milling around, but no one I recognize.

I plant myself on the sidelines and watch the barefoot boys kick a soccer ball made out of garbage bags and rubber bands. At each end of the red dirt is a goalpost made from three tree limbs nailed together. It looks like the boys are disputing whether the ball has gone offsides, but there are no borders to the field. Everything is imaginary.

Well, I can play that game too. I can imagine. So I imagine that Marcella is on one side of me and our friend Sydni on the other. *Are you ready for the date?* Marcella asks.

What are you going to wear? Sydni inquires.

Have you told your father? Marcella asks.

I'm smiling, thinking about going out with Isaiah, but they're so excited for me that I don't even have a chance to answer their questions. *I bet he's going to plant a big kiss right there.* Sydni points to my lips, when I feel a tug on my wrist.

"Hello!" Innocent says. He smiles and *pop*, a dimple puckers on each cheek. I snap out of my daydream. I'm here at Mzanga Full Primary, but at least I'm not alone.

Two of Innocent's little friends are at his side. Innocent points to the boy with cheeks as big as apples. "Silvester," he says. Then he points to the boy with almond-shaped eyes and says, "Abel."

"Hi," I say. "I'm Clare."

Silvester and Abel point at my face. I bend down. "What is it?" I ask.

The boys jab dots in the air with their fingers—poke, poke, poke. Soon the three of them go wiggly with laughter. *Did I leave some breakfast on my face? Do I have a zit?* I reach up and feel my nose. But it's smooth as satin.

"Oh," I say, and chuckle. While Dad is tall, dark, and Jewish, Mom was a redheaded, freckle-faced Catholic. I get my spray of freckles from her. She always said they give me personality. "Blood of the Irish!" I tell the boys, but they just look at me cross-eyed. So I stand up straight and proud, point to my nose, and try not to think about Mom anymore. I try not to think about how her skin was the color of peaches and cream, how she'd smell like rain after her bath. Instead, I point to the dots on my own nose and say, "Freckles."

"Ooh!" they say, fascinated by the extraordinary information. "Frrrreeeeckles."

Mr. Special Kingsley walks past us and shakes the bell in his hand. Immediately, the soccer game stops. Hundreds of kids scatter to class, kicking up dry red dirt like a hurricane. Suddenly, my blood swooshes in my ears, and the hustle and shuffle fades farther away.

I forget where I am. Forget where to go.

My heart's pounding when a little hand grabs mine and drags me from the field to the school building. We reach the standard eight door. A brown and white chicken struts inside, where my classmates are busy unpacking school supplies from their plastic grocery bags: notebooks torn in half across the middle and tiny pencil stubs. *"Zikomo,"* I tell Innocent. "*Zikomo* very much." Mrs. Tomasi isn't in the classroom yet, but Memory and Agnes are.

"Good morning!" Memory says as she moves off the wooden bench to let me in. Agnes is busy talking to the boy with the Florida-shaped scar on his hand, who sits at the table in front of us.

"Agnes comes to school exclusively to find husband," Memory explains. "Husband who own fancy shop in city."

The chicken pecks at my feet.

"I come to school to beat you," Agnes says to Memory. "Next term I shall be number one."

A girl sitting in the front of the classroom turns in her seat. She's stocky like a locust. She yells out something in Chichewa, her eyes full of horror.

"Patuma, you read," Agnes calls to her. "Maybe you shall be number three student someday. But not yet. Please do not worry about the American girl. We need not impress her."

"All you girls fight for me. I shall declare a winner soon," says the boy with the scarred hand. His fingers are extra-long and thin, and his eyes sparkle like he just stepped out of a swimming pool. "Winnie and Sickness shall fight for me as well."

Two girls, one with bulbous cheeks and another with silver hoop earrings, turn at the sound of their names. Both of them look healthy to me.

"Yes, let it be known. I shall be a very rich man," the boy tells me. "Do you know I sell reeds in the trading center on the weekend days? You may like to buy some for your roof."

"This boy is called Saidi," Memory explains.

Agnes holds her hands over her heart and bats her eyelashes. "Memory adore Saidi, but Saidi love only Agnes. It is what you call the love web."

"Love triangle?" I say.

"Love triangle," Memory says, and laughs. "What do I tell you? Agnes is not here to learn language of English."

"Only language of love," Agnes says.

Mrs. Tomasi wanders in. Today she's wearing a light purple print dress. She looks exactly like a lilac in spring. Since I have hay fever plus a really good imagination, the power of suggestion is pretty strong. The second I see her, I sneeze.

Mrs. Tomasi walks over to our table and hands me a piece of paper with Chichewa vocabulary words and English translations. The words are written out by hand. "Clare, you must copy each word five times. I shall quiz you tomorrow," she says. She heads to the front of the room, sits down at her metal folding table, and summons my classmates. One at a time, they kneel in front of our teacher as she quizzes them on their English vocabulary words.

Meanwhile, back at my bench, I copy over *sukulu*, which means "school," and *mbandakucha*, which means "early morning before sunrise, between first and third rooster." When Agnes returns from being quizzed, she stares at my paper. I lift it to my face so she can't see what I've written, but she inches even closer. "I see you have a magic pencil," she says. "A pencil that draws letters in color."

It's nice, I guess, but I certainly have better. "It's just a red Pilot pen," I say.

I set down my paper and try to keep copying my words, but it's totally impossible to focus. Agnes won't stop talking. "Most certainly a student in Malawi does not need a magic pencil unless she is at secondary school," she says, and holds out her hand, palm up. "I shall score highest on the Primary School Leaving Exam of the entire district. It is most certain I shall go to best secondary school in all Malawi. Therefore, you may give this magic pencil to me."

I try to ignore her as well as I can ignore someone who is superglued to my side. But when she keeps chattering, I decide that maybe this gift will make her leave me alone. Besides, I have plenty of pens in my bag. "Here," I say, and hand it over.

Agnes's eyes go wide and she smiles. "Saidi," she calls as he strolls back from Mrs. Tomasi's desk. "A magic pencil! Look!" Agnes grabs my vocabulary sheet and writes her name on the bottom of the paper in big red letters. "Put my name!" Saidi says. Without even asking, Agnes tears off the bottom of my worksheet to write Saidi's name too.

After quizzes, it's time for chores. Mrs. Tomasi orders Memory and Gloria to distribute the schoolbooks to the classrooms, she tells Winnie and Stella to chase the frazzled chicken outside, and she says that Agnes and Patuma must sweep the floor. As for Norman, Handlebar, Saidi, and the rest of the boys, they're sent to chop grass. But what about me? I'm full of dread. I wonder what on earth my sentence will be. Scrubbing? Chopping? Sweeping? As it turns out, though, I'm not ready for a complete sentence. "Right now, you must study words for the quiz tomorrow," my teacher says.

"Words? What about chores?" I ask.

Even though there's no such thing as a stupid question back at my school in Massachusetts, apparently here at Mzanga Full Primary School there is. Mrs. Tomasi cups her hand over her mouth and giggles. "You are an American girl, Clare. American girls need not do chores."

At that news, I breathe a sigh of relief louder than the first, second, and third roosters combined. But my good feeling only lasts as long as a blink, because then Mrs. Tomasi steps out of the classroom, and a blink after that, Agnes sweeps a cloud of red dust into my face.

CHAPTER 14

Once my coughing fit passes, I glare at Agnes and follow Memory outside. All the classes are lined up in the field for the daily assembly. It's easy to see that there are hundreds of little kids in this school and not nearly as many big ones. I ask Memory why. "Drop out due to illness, harvest, family members who need care," she says.

Mr. Special Kingsley calls for our attention and everyone sings the Malawi national anthem in English and Chichewa. Since I don't know the song, I use one of Marcella's tricks and mouth "watermelon, banana, watermelon, banana" over and over again, and it looks like I'm singing all the right words in both languages.

Mr. Special Kingsley makes the morning announcements: "The bricks for the new teacher house have dried. Standard six students shall start building this very afternoon. Further, there is word that a stray leopard has been spotted near a village on the other side of the district. Please take care not to wander into the bush."

This piece of news sends everyone, teachers included, tittering with excitement. It sets me chomping on my necklace in fright. And of course, Agnes is so ferocious she makes a leopard seem tame. Back in the classroom, she and Memory lean over me to read the story of Cinderella from the book we share. Agnes points to the picture of Cinderella at the ball with the handsome prince. "This beautiful girl is me." She flips backward a few pages to the picture of the ugly stepsisters and points to the one with the missing teeth. "You," Agnes tells Memory. And then to the one with the wart on her nose. "Glorious Blessing," she says to me, and giggles, "this girl is you."

"You are much worst than a stepsister," Memory tells Agnes. "You . . . you are a—" But Memory never gets to hurl her insult, because Mrs. Tomasi interrupts. She calls on Agnes to read out loud. I don't know how she does it, but Agnes flips right back to the page with Cinderella on it and reads two whole pages without making a single mistake. "A most magnificent performance," Mrs. Tomasi says.

My nostrils flare like a bloody bull's.

During social studies we go outside, where Mrs. Tomasi helps us paint a giant Malawian flag on an old sheet. After we leave the sheet to dry in the sun, we each gather small rocks for math. Our collections of rocks clatter onto our tables. I'm tempted to throw one at Agnes, but she's so skinny, it would probably crack one of her bones.

"Two-fifths is the same as what part of twenty?" Mrs. Tomasi asks. The room sounds like thunder as we all move our rocks around and try to figure out the answer. Handlebar raises his hand first. "Eight," he says.

"Correct," our teacher says. She gives us the next problem.

But I've got a problem all my own: this morning Dad said he wouldn't be able to leave the hospital to drive me home in the afternoon. "Amputation," he said. "But I'm confident you can find the way back from now on." I have to admit it's true. It's kind of tough to get lost since there's only one turn to make between the house and school, and there will be hundreds of kids walking in the same direction. I can't explain to Dad, though, that getting lost is not what I'm worried about.

Who I'm going to walk with this afternoon is.

Of course, I'd like to walk with Memory, but I haven't known her very long at all and she already has so many friends, and I'm sure I need her more than she needs me. So after math, I finally work up the guts and ask. *"Chabwino!"* she says, and smiles. "We shall meet on the hilltop after I gather the schoolbooks and my brother." Even though Innocent is dismissed earlier in the day, he sticks around to play soccer, make bricks, and walk home with his sister.

I'm still swimming in the sensation of sweet relief that I won't be walking by myself when I meet Memory and Innocent at the top of the hill fifteen minutes after Mrs. Tomasi dismisses us for the day. "How do you do that?" I ask Memory, staring at the box on her head.

Innocent walks between us, kicking a small rock like it's a soccer ball.

"Do what?" she says.

"The box. How do you keep it up there on your head?"

Memory laughs. "It is not much difficult." She takes it off her head. There's a red cloth ring beneath it. "Try," she says.

Memory puts the ring on my head, and then the box. I feel like I'm going to get crushed right into the ground. "Now you must walk."

I hold my breath. I've got one foot in the air when I hear laughter from the other side of the road. No sooner do I shoot a quick glance to see who's there than the box wobbles.

Memory and Innocent both reach out their arms. Memory catches the box before it smashes her brother.

"Sorry!" I shout.

Across the dirt road, three little girls imitate my spastic attempt to carry the box on my head.

"Perhaps a bit more practice may do you well," Memory says. "I shall carry the box for today." She places it back on top of her head. Then the three of us continue on past the tobacco farms, the ladies with machetes, and a herd of cows busily lapping rainwater from a puddle.

When we reach the path to my house, I take another look at her head. "Are you sure you don't have a secret shelf up there?"

Memory looks puzzled.

"Don't worry about it," I say, and wish her and Innocent a good afternoon.

I turn down the jungle path. A bunch of bright purple berries that I swear weren't here yesterday glimmer like small grapes in the dappled light. Overhead, a fat blue monkey with a fuzzy gray face plucks a melon from a vine and chomps away.

I'm thinking about how cute he looks when suddenly, he lifts the entire fruit over his head and chucks it to the ground beside me. Mud splatters all over my sneakers.

"*Watch it!*" I scream.

The dumb monkey *ooh-ooh-oohs*.

I run to the house. Mrs. Bwanali's out front unpinning clothes from the line. "Clare," she calls, "how is my girl?"

"Don't ask!" I say.

She sets Dad's blue hospital scrubs in the wicker basket, crosses the grass, and takes my hands. "I must ask. Are you hungry, love?"

I nod.

"Let Mrs. Bwanali fix your meal."

"*Zikomo,*" I say, and follow her inside.

I change out of my uniform, grab my sketchpad. Then I plunk down on the kitchen chair and draw that naughty little primate. When I cough, Mrs. Bwanali boils water for tea and sings me a tune in Chichewa.

"You know this song, Clare?"

I shake my head.

"It is a special song about a hungry boy who eat and eat. Yet this food is never enough. One day the hungry child fall down and the papa hug the boy, and the boy say, 'Now I am full.' The boy is not full with *nsima*. The boy is full with love."

CHAPTER 15

I wake up Saturday morning between the first and third rooster crow, and I can't fall back to sleep. How could I possibly? A whole entire weekend looms before me without the prospect of a single movie, trip to the Museum of Fine Arts, or visit to the mall. And even that I could survive. But a weekend without one friend? I burrow under the sheet. I've got nothing to do other than think, and no one to spend time with besides my father. I'd rather hang out with Mrs. Bwanali than Dad, but she doesn't work Saturdays or Sundays.

Dad rocks the house with his snores while I brush my teeth with bottled water and eat a banana and some *nsima* that's left in the fridge. Then I put on a T-shirt and shorts and weave tiny braids in half of my hair. I fasten the bottom of each one with elastics that are still at the bottom of my backpack from when I had my braces. I sketch for an hour out on the veranda, but then I'm bored with that. And by ten o'clock, I can feel my muscles literally itching to get out of the house, even though there's absolutely nowhere to go. So at 10:22, when my father gets up and walks out to the covered porch in his pajamas and says, "What do you say we go see some animals?" I nod a little too eagerly.

Dad smiles.

I want to tell him not to get excited—it's only because I'm so crazy bored my brain feels like it's about to explode right inside my skull—but that would require talking.

"I'm going to throw on some clothes, eat something quick—did you eat?"

I nod again.

"Super!" Dad says. "Then we'll head out to Liwonde National Park. You'll love it. It's great!"

An hour later, we've paid the fee at the gate. The attendant gives us a map of the park, a list of the animals we'll see, and a paper that says we shouldn't leave our vehicle under any circumstances. We're winding along the Shire River. I'm thinking that I'm almost used to riding in what would be the driver's seat in the United States when all of a sudden, I spot a six-foot-long lizard tanning on a rock and a bunch of crocodiles bathing in the lagoon. As the dirt road winds through the forest and across the savannah, seven warthogs snort their way right in front of the Land Rover. They are the ugliest things I've ever seen, but still, they take my breath away. There are vervet monkeys and antelopes too. For a while I can't help it, I'm saying "Wow!" and "Check that one out!" every other minute. Dad stops the car so I can sketch the African fish eagle and a waterbuck grazing on the tall grass.

I've just finished my drawing when Dad ruins everything. "Clare," he says, "I thought we could talk about how you're doing. About your mother."

I look at him. It's a trick. He's got me trapped.

He tries to put his arms around my shoulder. "I know how painful it is," he says.

And that's when I turn to him. Turn on him. He doesn't know how painful it is. He's over it. Over her. Obviously. He's dancing and smiling and laughing. He's back to normal and it hasn't even been a whole year. Isn't my mother worth at least a year of sadness, a year of pain? "You don't know!" I shout. "You don't even care anymore." I slam my fists against the dashboard, but I don't feel anything at all. And I don't feel the tears pouring down my face, yet I taste them when I try to catch my breath.

Suddenly, I don't care if I get eaten alive. I just need to get away from him, so I throw open the Land Rover door and run and run and run. As I run, I see too far into the distance. I see my life without Mom: my prom, my wedding, my kids. It will be just me and my dad, who doesn't even know me anymore.

"Clare!" Dad shouts. "Get back here!"

And then I see it. A python winding through the tree. My heart thumps in my throat. I grind to a halt. I'll be dead in seconds anyway.

Dad comes up behind me. I point.

"It's a vine," he says, and sighs. He squeezes my wrist and pulls me back to the Land Rover. Once we're inside, he locks the doors. Then he rests his forehead on the steering wheel and closes his eyes.

"Dad?" I say, but he doesn't move. *Is he furious? Is he having a heart attack? What's going on?* "Dad!" I shout.

He lifts his head. "You scared me," he whispers.

"Sorry."

"And Clare . . ."

"What?" A flock of tiny blackbirds circles the air.

"I miss your mother more than anything." He looks out the window. His shoulders shake. I watch him like that for a long time. I don't know what to do, what to say. I fit my molars into the dent in my pendant.

It's strange to be here with my dad crying. There's nowhere to run. Nowhere to hide. It's only the second time I've ever seen him cry. The first time was at Mom's funeral. I mean, everyone was crying there. It's a funeral. You're supposed to cry. But for some reason, I was the only person in the whole church who didn't. I couldn't. I'd cried so much already, I was exhausted.

A pack of impalas leaps across the grass in front of the Land Rover. I'm tempted to get out, run away with them. Even though I didn't want Dad to be happy without me, suddenly, I don't want him to be sad with me either. I mean, what is a girl supposed to do when her father's beside her melting down?

But then, as if she has heard my very thought, my mother appears. Not in pieces or flashes, but like a picture. Whole. "Make room for me," she says. I move over on the seat so she can fit next to the window. In an instant, I remember everything about her. About us. About how much she loves me and

80

*Dad. About how our family is supposed to work. I can't be-
lieve she's finally come.*

"Clare," she says, "he needs you."

"You're here," I say.

"Where else would I be?" she asks.

It's like not a day has passed, like she's never left us.

"Be there for your dad," she says. Her shimmering voice
sounds like a piece of sun. "Please."

"What do you mean?" I ask. "Be there how?"

"You're smart," Mom says, and smiles. "You'll find a way.
And one more thing."

*She looks radiant. She looks like she should be on a tele-
vision commercial for skin cream.* "Grief isn't a tunnel you
walk through and you're done," she says. "It waxes and wanes
like the moon." *She kisses me on the cheek. I smell the cold
cream on her face.*

I reach over and touch Dad's shoulder. "Grief isn't a
tunnel you walk through and you're done," I tell him.

Dad looks at me, his blue-gray eyes caught in a storm. I
hug him, and when I'm finished, my mother is gone.

On Sunday, I celebrate the fact that I didn't get torn to
shreds by a lion by transforming my bedroom into a place
where someone with a pulse can actually live. But what to
use? I rummage through the dresser and pull out seven
scarves. I collect scarves because Marcella told me that a
teenager can never accessorize too much. I tie them end to
end until I've got a bright strip of orange and gold swirls,
blue stars on purple, and rainbow stripes. I drape my

creation over the top of the dresser. The colors pour down each side. Next, I take a white T-shirt and stick all my earrings through it to make a dazzling splash. I put the T-shirt with my jewels on one of the six hangers in the house. And voilà!

Dad knocks on the door and says he wants to head over to the village and see his friends. He wants to know if I'd like to come.

"Notice anything different?" I ask.

But of course he doesn't. He's a man.

So I give him a little tour and he pretends to be impressed. "Very nice use of color palette and contrast," he says, although it's clear he's only throwing around words my mother and I always used. "And remember your hat," he says.

I feel warm inside. I can't believe Dad said that. I can't believe he told me to remember my hat. I put on a skirt, T-shirt, sandals, and of course, my Red Sox cap. It's a relief to be wearing something other than my school uniform.

When we get to Mkumba village, he walks with me to Memory's hut, where an old woman missing her front teeth comes to the door. She smiles and her eyes water. Then she kneels in front of my father and says, *"Moni, adokotala,"* and talks to my father in Chichewa.

"This is Memory's grandmother," Dad tells me.

"Moni," I say. Dad translates while Memory's grandma points to the river and says that Memory is there with her friends. I glance behind the hut and see their bright-colored dresses in the distance. "Why don't you go visit with them," Dad says. "I'm going to find Stallard. I'll meet you at the clearing before sundown."

"It's a plan," I say, and mosey down the path. I hope they don't mind me crashing their party. They've probably known each other since they were born. And now here I am needing some company. Why should they bother with me? I'll be flying back to the United States in two months anyway.

When I get closer to the river, I see that it's Sickness and Patuma there washing dishes with Memory. Sickness sees me. She smiles and says, "Visitor! Hello!"

The Malawian people are so polite and friendly. Even if they don't want you tagging along, you'd never know.

"Hey!" I say. No sooner do I reach the bank of the river than Sickness yells, "River battle!" And Memory fills a pot with water and throws it at me. At first I stand there, shocked. That's not polite. My hair is dripping and there's mud on my clothes. I think it might be some mistake. Maybe Memory tripped and fell.

But then Sickness says, "Go water her!" And she hands me the biggest pot she has. Well, I'm not one to refuse a good old water fight on a day as hot as this one, so I step into the river with my sandals still on, fill the pot, and dump it on Memory's head while Sickness holds her in place. Patuma's flat on her back on the bank, squealing with giggles as the rest of us splash each other until we're completely drenched and laughing till we cry.

Then we lie out in the field in our wet dresses and dry off in the sun like raisins, and talk about boys in a mixture of languages because Patuma's English is pretty bad and my Chichewa's almost nonexistent. By the end of the conversation, we've established a few basic facts: Memory not only loves Saidi, but she also plans to marry him one day.

Patuma loves Norman and Norman loves Patuma back, although they're both too shy to admit it.

"Do you date Norman?" I ask Patuma. Despite the sunscreen, my cheeks are really starting to burn.

"What is date?" Sickness asks.

So I explain and Memory says, "A Malawi girl do not do this thing called date. When a boy is ready to marry, he go to the villages and ask, 'Is there a girl in this village who can marry me?' Or, in the case that there is one certain girl the boy watch and know from school, he ask that girl. If the girl accept, the uncle of the boy shall meet with the parents of the girl to map the way forward. Then the wedding."

Sickness giggles and says, "The golden rule is if the boy and the girl meet in secret—for example, the boy find the girl down by the river as she do dishes or boy and girl talk much at school—this boy and girl must not allow the parents to discover the relationship."

Then Patuma pipes up in Chichewa, and Sickness explains, "Patuma say that even though she do not marry Norman yet, she look at Norman in the eye one time and Norman look right back at her. Patuma say this is how they talk in secret at school."

I glance through the leaves at the clouds gliding by and feel a pang in my chest, because I know my mother would love it here. No matter where we used to travel, she always found a way to escape into nature. In Quebec, while Dad attended lectures, Mom rented a scooter and we rode out to Mount Pinnacle and spent the day hiking. And the time he had a meeting in Miami, we took a moped out to Everglades National Park, where we picnicked and laughed at the alligators and turtles. I wonder if Memory thinks about her mother all the time too. I want to ask her, but I've only known her a week. How long do you need to know someone before you can ask the most painful question there is?

Soon our throats are itching with thirst, but the river water is too muddy to drink in the rainy season, and I didn't think to bring a water bottle with me. "Shall we fetch clean drinking water?" Sickness says.

And I say, "Of course! Why not!"

So the girls collect pails from their homes and Memory gives one to me. An hour after we set out for the borehole, we finally arrive. I don't think I can take another step, though, because my left foot has blistered by my ankle.

After we fill our buckets and gulp down some clean water for ourselves, Memory splits a plant leaf and rubs the gel inside it onto my blister, and then we head back. The moon is high in the sky. I'm surprised to see it there, like an unexpected visitor in the last light of day.

My arms tremble from the weight of one water bucket, even though the other girls each carry two—one on their heads and one in their hands. And when we finally return to the village, the sun is setting behind the curtain of the earth, so I say goodbye to my friends and meet my father in the clearing.

CHAPTER 16

Every cloud has a silver lining, but take it from me, if that cloud has a thunderbolt pointed straight at your head, the silver lining won't give you much comfort.

Monday morning I decide I might actually come out of this whole adventure alive. But by the afternoon, I reconsider. During science class, Mrs. Tomasi puts a bunch of materials on each table: a single leaf, a strip of brown bark, and a yellowish oval-shaped melon that's about the size of a cantaloupe. I'm tempted to eat it. My stomach is growling. No matter how big a breakfast Mrs. Bwanali makes me or how much water I drink during the day when no one's looking, I don't think I'll ever get used to eating lunch after school. I pick up the different things. The fruit has a rough circle where the stem was attached to the tree. The leaf is cool and smooth. And the bark is wrinkly, like an old man's skin.

While we feel the parts of the tree, Mrs. Tomasi tells us that the fruit of the baobab tree has more vitamin C than an orange. "If there is a drought," she says, "you can cut the trunk of a baobab tree and suck out seven thousand five hundred liters of water with a grass straw. This tree can live for thousands of years and grow twelve meters in diameter. Sometimes people live right inside the trunks."

"Cool!" I say.

Memory nods in agreement.

When the school bell chimes, we gather our science materials and carry them up front. Memory sets the baobab fruit on Mrs. Tomasi's folding table and picks up the large cardboard box that's on the floor in the corner. "Innocent and myself shall meet you on the hilltop in quarter hour," she tells me. She leaves the classroom behind Saidi, Agnes, Patuma, and the others while I go back to my seat and pull out my sketchbook to pass the time.

After Mrs. Tomasi wipes the vegetable chalk off the board with a rag, she collects her notebook and pencil. "*Yendani bwino,*" she says. That's one of the phrases I got right on my quiz yesterday. It means "Have a safe journey." In fact, the only word I missed was *utawaleza*. It means "rainbow," but for some reason I thought it meant "grain silo."

I wave to Mrs. Tomasi. "*Yendani bwino* to you too," I say.

The second Mrs. Tomasi leaves, a cold wind blows through the classroom and the hair on my arms stands up straight. Something doesn't feel right, though I have no idea what it could be, other than I've got to sit here in this classroom alone for the next fifteen minutes. But what's so

87

scary about that? *Chill!* I tell myself. I try to breathe in love and breathe out fear, which is what Marcella does before she goes onstage, but it doesn't work. Instead, I draw a picture of Agnes as a *bongololo*.

When I'm done, I grab my backpack and head outside. Innocent and Memory are halfway up the hill, and all the textbooks owned by Mzanga Full Primary are in a box on top of Memory's head. I'm only a few feet outside the classroom when suddenly, the wind howls and the trees sway. Then, *crack!* A bolt of lightning strikes the ground right in front of my feet. I tremble from head to toe. Memory and Innocent turn to race back down the hill to school. "Over here!" I shout through the wind. There's a train pulling into a station—a station inside my head! And I'm not sure if they can see me. Except for the flashes of bright white light, suddenly, it's as dark as night.

I hurry back to my classroom and wait for Memory and Innocent while the air blinks like a strobe light and water drips—*splat! splat! splat!*—through the small holes in the ceiling. Good thing Mrs. Tomasi keeps a stack of empty cans in the corner. I grab them and put one beside the doorway, one on my table, one by the board. Soon I'm out of cans but not out of leaks.

The rain thunders down. My thoughts crash into each other, totally out of control. *Where is Memory? Where is Innocent? Why aren't they here?*

Boom!

I scream.

Aiiee!

I can't hear my scream. That terrifies me, makes me scream more.

I run to the doorway. Through flashes of lightning, I see a huge sheet of metal. It cuts across the field, shiny like a bullet.

My sneakers slosh through a puddle until I see where the metal came from—the standard five block. My pulse thunders in my ears. The roof flew right off the classroom, sharp and dangerous like a weapon.

The rain turns to mist while mosquitoes whine all around me. Thousands band together in big black clouds. Mosquito armies attack my arms and legs. I slap them away. They come right back. Questions bite me all over: *Where is Memory? Where is Innocent? Is anyone hurt? Is anyone dead?*

The mosquitoes are ferocious! They claw me, pinch me, pierce me. I whimper as I scratch. I plead with them to stop, but they won't. I run to a banana tree and scratch my back against the bark. I stay there quivering and sobbing until finally, the thunder stops, the lightning stops, and the sun showers down and convinces the critters to find another source of blood.

Then it's over.

But inside, the storm doesn't stop: *Where is Memory? Where is Innocent? Is anyone hurt? Is anyone dead?*

Out of nowhere, I hear a voice. *"Wabalarika eti?"* I look up.

Saidi is holding a ball made of garbage bags and string. "Are you scared and confused?" he asks.

I nod. My brain is whipping around like sugar in a cotton candy machine.

"I am sorry to tell you, Clare . . ."

I brace myself for the worst. The very worst.

"Upon my exit from the shelter of the standard three classroom where I waited for the rains to leave, I examine the situation with a great and careful eye," he says.

I quake with fear.

"Yes, it is true," Saidi says.

"What? What's true?" I ask.

"*Bongololo* bugs are dead now on floor." He smiles. "Do not worry, Clare. There was no person in standard five block. No person on the field in this place. No teacher. No children. Only *bongololo* bugs. You cry for *bongololo*?"

I shake my head no and swat an evil mosquito from my arm. Got him!

Then I spot Innocent walking toward us, Memory behind him. I choke out a sob. They're drenched. We all are. Innocent's teeth chatter. Memory rubs his back, tries to warm him up. We meet in the tall patch of field grass, all of us scratching our bites like mad.

"Don't cry," I tell Memory. "Everyone's okay," I say. "It's only the *bongololo* that's hurt." I chuckle through my tears.

"I do not cry," she says, and quickly wipes her cheek with the back of her hand. "The rains soaked the books is the problem. The box rip in the rains. I forget the plastic bag for the box. We run to standard one room. It is more near."

Memory looks at the ground and turns silent. Innocent and Saidi do the same. "Thank you, Lord, who keep the children of Mzanga safe. We beg of you, our parents, our Lord: protect our books. We leave them to dry in sun behind standard one classroom block. Please do not allow the thief to steal them in the night. We do thank the spirit of *amayi* and *abambo*, our mother and father, for seeing us through the difficult rains," she says.

My heart stops. All of a sudden, I get it. This is a prayer. A prayer to Memory's mother. And her father! They're both dead. Gone. It's too terrible to imagine. I want to ask Memory how she does it. How she survives. But then Saidi says, "Enough tears, my friends," and my chance is gone.

Saidi tosses his garbage-bag ball to Innocent and says, "Let us have some fun." The ball crunches as Innocent catches it. He throws the ball back to Saidi, who dribbles it on his head as he leaps away over the puddles back to his soccer game. Mr. Special Kingsley and teachers walk out of the headmaster's office. Mr. Special Kingsley and two of the teachers circle the field, checking on students. The rest of the teachers gather around the roof. It looks like they're trying to figure out what to do with it.

And even though Memory and Innocent no longer need to drop the books off at the trading center, they will still walk past the turnoff to my house on their way to Mkumba village. So together we scratch our bites and trudge up the muddy hill. Heat shimmies off puddles, turning the schoolyard into a foggy dream. When we get to the top, there it is, arching gracefully over the muddy road: *utawaleza*—a little bow of God. The rainbow is bright and vibrant. I'm sure we'll walk right through it on our way back, but we never even get close.

At home, Mrs. Bwanali greets me with sugared tea and boiled pumpkin. After I cover myself in calamine lotion from head to toe, I sit at the table and draw scenes of the storm: a can catching leaks, the ripped book box, the roof in the field.

When I tell Mrs. Bwanali how awful it all was, she throws a dish towel over her shoulder and turns to me. "Clare, it is the rains that bring us flowers. A life without rains is ugly and dull."

I sip my tea. I know what she means, but still, I didn't like the storm.

CHAPTER 17

E ven though Mrs. Bwanali walks to the house in the
mornings, Dad insists on driving her home when
she's finished with work. She always tells him she isn't
tired, but we can just look at her face and see that she's
exhausted.

One evening after Dad gets back from driving Mrs.
Bwanali home to Kapoloma village, he calls through the
veranda that I should come outside. "Got a present for
you, Clare!" Ever since our visit to the game park, things
have been much better between us.

As I pull on my sandals, I wonder what Dad's gift could
be. A set of paints? A poster for my wall? I run outside.
"So, how do you like her?" he says, holding up an old black
bicycle that doesn't have a kickstand. It looks like the one
Saidi rides to school.

"Awesome!" I say.

"Yeah, I figured now that you're a teenager, you might like a little freedom. She's rickety but she'll get you down to the village, and back and forth to school."

I touch the black tape on the handlebars and look for the gears. "How many speeds?" I ask.

"Oh, uh, just one," Dad says.

"That's okay. It's perfect!" I say, and hug him. "Where'd you get it?"

Dad strokes the stubble on his chin. "Someone left it behind."

"Behind where?" I ask.

"You know, at the hospital." Dad checks out the stars winking in the baby blue sky.

"Well, did they say you could have it?"

"Oh, yeah, yeah," he says, and sighs. "My patient won't be needing it anymore."

I shiver. I don't really want to ride a dead person's bike. Then I sneeze.

"You okay?" Dad asks.

"Just exhausted, and my throat sort of hurts." I've been tired ever since we got here. "When is this jet lag going away?" I ask. Besides, I don't want to tell him his gift is giving me the creeps.

"It's probably allergies," Dad says. "Those'll wipe you out."

Dad puts his arm around me and we go inside, where he looks down my throat and up my nose with a flashlight and says, "Yup, allergies. Nothing to worry about."

We light the oven to heat up the chicken Mrs. Bwanali made earlier, but before the chicken's even cooked, the electricity goes out. Once again, we have to change our dinner plans at the last minute. Instead, we eat leftover *nsima* and cold pumpkin by candlelight, and I ask Dad more about his work.

"The Global Health Project can't keep up with all the disease here," he says. "There are cockroaches climbing on the hospital beds and walls, so that doesn't help matters. There's not enough medicine. Today a boy came in with a violin spider bite. Flesh on the leg was rotting. I had no hydrogen peroxide—had to clean the wound with a rag and a bottle of vodka. He may need an amputation."

I put down my fork of cold pumpkin.

"The life expectancy is only fifty-three here," he says. "Can you believe that?"

Well, my mother was only forty-four when she died. And she lived in one of the richest countries in the world: the United States of America. And I still can't believe that! I feel my eyes bursting like little plastic bags full of water, the kind I used to take home from the school carnival with goldfish inside. My chair screeches against the floor. I run through the minuscule living room to my bedroom and climb under the malaria net in the dark.

When Dad comes in, he apologizes. "I'm sorry, honey. I didn't realize that would upset you so much."

"It's not your fault," I say. And it's not. Not his fault that my mother died. Not his fault that he brought me here. Not his fault that in a country like this, kids with dead parents are a dime a dozen. "I love you," I tell Dad. A breeze blows through the window screen and ruffles the net like a sail.

For the rest of the week, Dad drives me to school, because I just can't get behind riding a dead person's bicycle. It doesn't seem right. And besides, I have other plans for this piece of machinery. Dad agreed right away to let me do it, so this weekend, I'm going to give the old bike a brand-new life.

On Friday, after assembly, I've just begun walking back to class with Memory and telling her about my plan when our headmaster appears beside me.

"Clare," he says, "may I have a word?"

"Yeah," I say. "I mean, yes, sir." As if I have a choice!

Memory runs ahead to catch up with Patuma and Winnie.

As Mr. Special Kingsley talks, he limps across the schoolyard, away from my classroom. "Clare," he says, "the District Education Office is always troubled to supply teachers in the bush. The assignments in cities are sought after, but here, we do not have the housing. Many teachers do not speak our tribal languages. Even though the request for the standard one replacement was sent months ago when the teacher married and became full with child, the District Education Office cannot find a teacher to send to the country. All the young teachers want a city placement. Zomba. Blantyre. Lilongwe. Yes! But the bush? 'No zikomo!' they say. One and the next and the next."

While Mr. Special Kingsley babbles on, kids lean out of classroom windows to gape at us. The American girl and the headmaster together, after classes have already begun? Clearly something unusual is going on.

"The other day, the standard one teacher and her new

husband and the girl child moved to Kenya, the homeland of the husband. We are improving as a nation. Yes, this is true. And every student here at Mzanga Full Primary must do a part. I have been filling in the lessons myself, but it is not a practical consideration for the headmaster to do so for each and every subject."

My throat closes as it occurs to me what this is all about: Agnes has ratted on me. She must have found Mr. Special Kingsley during chore time and told him it isn't fair that I get to study vocabulary words instead of sweep the floor just because I'm American.

"I shall like to request for you to teach the English to the standard one children," Mr. Special Kingsley says. "One hour each morning while your standard eight classmates practice their English reading."

"Teach?" I say. "I can't . . . sir . . . I, uh, I don't know how!"

"It would be my great honor for you to educate these students," he says. "Only until the district sends a replacement. As I explained, the teacher has moved to Kenya with her new family."

"How . . . why . . . ?" I can't even string a sentence together, never mind teach English to kids who only speak a few words of it.

Mr. Special Kingsley dabs his forehead with his handkerchief. "Clare, I ask you to help our school."

"But I'm just thirteen years old," I say. "I'm barely even a teenager, sir!"

"Many of our assistants are younger than you, Clare. I shall be teaching the remaining subjects to the students myself. However, I shall need a moment each morning to tend to my other responsibilities. I cannot teach and run the school all at the same time."

"I don't know, sir," I say. After all, it isn't my fault that the standard one teacher up and left in the middle of the school year.

"Clare, please ponder this request during the weekend. Bring me your answer at assembly Monday morning. I promise you, Clare, I shall understand your choice, no matter if it bring flood or flower."

As I cross the field back to the standard eight room, the water level rises higher and higher in my mind. There's going to be a mighty flood all right! Sure, the standard one students behave when Mr. Special Kingsley is around, but what will happen when he isn't? Chances are I'll be covered in spitballs in five minutes flat.

Memory loves the plan, so Saturday morning, I fill my backpack with wire hangers, a bottle of water, an umbrella, a wrench from Dad's tool kit, and some medical tape, although Dad will only give me a tiny bit. He says it's too valuable in the hospital.

I walk the bicycle over to Mkumba village, where Memory is outside bathing Innocent. As soon as Innocent sees me, he jumps out of the tub and runs into the hut to put on his clothes.

Memory and I wheel the bike through the village in search of Saidi. Once we find him, we explain the plan, and then the three of us mosey back to Memory's place so Innocent can help us build our invention.

Behind the hut we find two orange plastic basins, which we'll use for the container. Then Memory and I unscrew the bolts from the bike frame. Meanwhile, Innocent holds one of the basins still for Saidi, who pierces holes in the bottom of it with his pocketknife. The whole time we're working, Innocent is yapping up a storm in Chichewa.

Once Memory and I finally wrangle off the front bicycle tire, Saidi begins an interrogation: "Clare, a most important question: Innocent want to discover why you, Glorious Blessing, visit standard one room in the morning hour with the headmaster yesterday."

Of course, I already told Memory all about this, and she promised she wouldn't tell anyone else until I made up my mind for sure. But now it seems the cat is out of the bag. "If you can believe this one," I say, and chuckle, because I still can't believe it myself, "Mr. Special Kingsley asked me to teach English to Innocent's class until the District Education Office sends a regular teacher. He said I can let him know Monday whether I'll take the job."

Innocent starts blabbering to Saidi in Chichewa again, so I get back to work. My plan is to use the hanger to secure the orange plastic basins to the bicycle frame, but the wire is too stiff to maneuver.

Memory says she has a better idea. I follow her to a nearby *mombo* tree, where she peels some thread right off the bark! Back at the hut, we pull the hanger out of the hole in the basin and use the tree thread instead to secure the basin to the bicycle seat.

Memory and I are admiring our progress when Saidi

interrupts. "Innocent offer good deal to you, Glorious Blessing. I suggest you answer yes."

"A deal? What are you," I ask, "his lawyer?"

Saidi ignores me. "Here is deal," he says. "All visitors to Malawi must see our beautiful Lake Malombe with fish of all colors. Have you seen this lake?"

I shake my head no.

"Good, good. This is good," Saidi says.

"It is?" I weave the tree thread through the hole in the second plastic tub. This basin will be the cover. "Why is this good?" I ask.

"Good because Innocent give promise," Saidi says. "Innocent shall take you to lake, if you give promise back to Innocent. You can win this trip to Lake Malombe if you agree to teach English to standard one students. Innocent say that Mr. Special Kingsley is . . ." Saidi looks at Memory and yawns extra loud.

"Boring," Memory says.

I crouch down to look Innocent in the eyes. I don't bother to tell him that some people, like movie stars and teachers, are born to take center stage, and that I'm definitely not one of them. Instead, I say, "I will seriously consider your offer." While Saidi translates my words, I cringe with guilt, because I'm a rotten liar. I already know the answer. Sure, I can babysit. But teach a whole class? No way!

CHAPTER 18

I'm on the couch staring at the ceiling, replaying the conversation with Innocent over and over again in my mind, when Dad gets back from the hospital. He's wearing his blue hospital scrubs and clogs. "So, I was thinking more about what you told me last night," he says, "about Mr. Kingsley's request."

"And it's crazy!" I say. "I mean, it's probably against the law to ask a kid to teach."

"For money, maybe, but as a volunteer, probably not," Dad says. "Plus, your mom was a teacher before you were born, you know."

"Of course I know that," I say. I've heard the story a million times. Dad was sitting in the Coffee Connection on Harvard Street, moaning and groaning as he tried to figure out what to write for his essay on the application to medical school. Mom was at the next table correcting student papers, trying to figure out what was wrong with the man beside her. Finally, she leaned over and said, "Excuse me. Do you need a doctor?" And when Dad told her what was the matter, they both laughed until Dad was snorting and Mom had tears running down her cheeks. The rest, as they say, is history.

"I'm not Mom," I tell Dad. I mean, she was better than me in so many ways. She could speak in front of a class or at a gallery opening, no problem. She could go into a room full of strangers and leave with five best friends.

"I know you're not her," he says, and steps into his bedroom to change. "But you do have a lot in common. Just sayin'."

So I lie there on the couch and imagine my mother teaching her fourth-grade students to read and write, which she did until I was born and she decided to pursue her art full-time. I think about Innocent, how his eyes smiled when I told him I'd consider teaching his class. And I think there's a reason I work behind the scenes in the school theater, sewing costumes and designing sets for real actresses like Marcella.

Then I doze off.

I dream I'm at the Franklin Park Zoo on a sunny fall afternoon. Sunlight sparkles through the trees. Mom and I walk down the cobblestone path holding hands. Dead leaves crunch under our shoes until we stop at a dark green bench in front of the flamingo pool. We sit there hand in hand and watch the funny pink birds. I rest my head against her shoulder. "Don't be afraid," Mom says.

"But it's—it's not me," I stutter. "I can't."

"You're not who you used to be," she tells me. "Not anymore."

Dad comes down the path wearing hospital scrubs and a tall yellow hat, but then I realize that he isn't who he used to be either. He's the Man with the Yellow Hat from the Curious George books I used to read as a kid. "Come on," the Man with the Yellow Hat says. "Let's feed the lions."

"Go ahead," Mom says. "I'm too tired to move."

"Be right back," I say, and unthread my fingers from hers. I follow the Man with the Yellow Hat to the lion cage. The cage is a huge mosquito net hanging from a cloud. There are hundreds of lions roaring and snarling. My heart is pounding. I can't breathe.

"They're just hungry for their food," the man says. "Don't be scared."

"Do they want to eat me?" I ask, trembling.

"No," says the Man with the Yellow Hat. "Not today, anyway." He laughs and pushes over a wheelbarrow. The basket on it is bright orange and full of scraps of raw meat. "Hold on," the man says, and I squeeze the familiar handles. Suddenly, I'm inside the cage with the Man with the Yellow Hat. "You can do this," he assures me.

And I do. I can't believe it, but I do.

I dish out food to the lions. They look like beasts but they have human faces. Faces of children. One lets me pet him. Another lets me ride on her back. I'm having so much fun that I almost forget my mother, until I remember. I remember what I almost forgot. "My mother!" I gasp. "Let me out!"

Frantic, I run back to the bench. It's been hours. My mom is gone. I scream and run around the zoo past all the animals, but I can't find her anywhere. Then I look at the sky, at the moon. "You know what to do," says the Man in the Moon.

"I do?" I ask.

The Man in the Moon winks and says, "You do."

CHAPTER 19

When I get to school Monday morning, there's some kind of drama going on near the soccer field. All the players are crowded around the edge of the field. And kids big and small are gathered in a giant knot. When I get to the bottom of the hill, Winnie runs over and tells me what the fuss is about. "Memory bring the book in a traveling washbasin," she says. Winnie's eyes are wild with excitement. "No one can believe! You shall have to move through the students to glimpse."

I laugh. Of course, I already know what this incredible invention looks like. And I'm glad everyone thinks the bookmobile is as cool as I do. Now Memory can take our schoolbooks back and forth from the trading center without worrying about them getting wet or ripping in the rains. And finally the top of her head can have a rest too.

When Mr. Special Kingsley shakes the school bell, the

crowd breaks up, and I see Memory wheel our invention across the grass. She's grinning brighter than the midday sun. Who knew that an old bicycle and two cracked plastic washbasins could bring so much joy? Those old basins were no good for bathing anymore, but we patched them up with Dad's medical tape, and now they work great. One tub holds the books, and the other works as the cover to protect the books from the rain.

I catch up to Memory as she parks the bookmobile behind our classroom. Then we go inside and settle onto our bench. Mrs. Tomasi's busy talking to Oscar and Norman up front, and everything's fine until Agnes leans across me to tell Memory, "Only a girl whose arms bend like the palm leaf in the breeze cannot carry her load without special assistant." Suddenly, Memory shoves me, and without thinking, I automatically bang into Agnes, who falls right off the edge of the bench onto the floor.

"Brilliant!" I tell Memory. No sooner do I raise my palm to high-five Memory than Saidi runs over to help Agnes up off the floor, while Mrs. Tomasi glares at us, unsure of what to make of the strange scene.

The truth is, no matter what Agnes has said to Memory, the whole time I'm copying over my new vocabulary words, I'm the one whose arms are bending like a palm leaf in the breeze. And not only my arms, but also my legs and my whole entire body. Yes, I'm furious at Agnes for insulting Memory, but also I'm terrified. What I'm about to do is crazy! When Mr. Special Kingsley finds me after assembly, I force myself to spill the news.

"Clare," he says, and grins. "You are a brave lion. This I know all along."

I look at Mr. Special Kingsley sideways. First, I'm not brave. I'm shaking from head to toe, and sweat is dripping down my armpits. Second, what an odd choice of words, because the first lesson I've planned is called Animal Bingo. The idea popped into my brain after I woke up from my nap on Saturday. The goal is to teach students the English names of different animals.

After I thought of it, I spent hours making forty Bingo cards. Each one has nine squares and each square has an animal sketch inside. I sketched snakes, dogs, cats, lions, monkeys, and bears. Then I cut up paper into tiny pieces so the students can place the pieces on top of the squares on the Bingo cards. By last night, I had used up an entire sketchpad, and my hand was throbbing, it was so sore.

I follow my headmaster into the standard one classroom. Innocent smiles up at me from the floor. *Hello, Dimples!* And I think that all my work preparing for this lesson was worth it.

Before I can get started, though, Mr. Special Kingsley wants to make a formal introduction. He wipes his forehead with his handkerchief and speaks to the kids in Chichewa. They jump up, throw back their shoulders, and belt out a welcome song for me. As they sing, I count them. *One, two, three . . . thirty-seven, thirty-eight, thirty-nine.* I'm not even halfway through counting when I get a sick feeling. I don't have nearly enough Bingo cards.

I do a quick scan of the floor and gulp. There are at least a hundred and twenty students in this room! Even if they work in pairs, there aren't enough cards to share. And their song is almost through. If I can't teach them to play Animal Bingo, then what on earth am I supposed to do? As the song ends and the students sit back down, I turn around to ask Mr. Special Kingsley this question, but he's gone. Never mind bending in the breeze like a palm leaf, I must have been hit on the head with a coconut. What was I thinking!

I make a break for it but Innocent beats me. He stretches his arms and legs as wide as he can across the doorway to block my escape. Over Innocent's shoulder I spot our headmaster, a small blue dot strolling back to his office. Innocent's bright pink bottom lip rolls over. He furrows his brow. "*Freckles!*" he shouts.

"What?" I croak.

"Freckles!" say more than a hundred students who sit side by side on the cracked concrete floor grinning at me, shiny white teeth against shiny black skin.

I really need to sit down, but surprise surprise, there isn't a chair anywhere in sight. Instead, I cough and cough. For a minute, I can't stop. Innocent issues his order again: "Freckles!"

I grab my heart pendant and grind my teeth into the dent.

And suddenly, here's my mother. All of her. She's wrapped in her green bathrobe, pointing to her face. "Freckles, Clare," she says, as if I've gone thick in the head. "You know, these things. My beauty marks. And yours." She dots her finger across her own face.

I stare in disbelief.

"Teach the children freckles," she says. "It's simple, really."
Then she laughs a fluttery laugh, like an elm leaf spiraling to

the ground in a breeze. There's no doubt about it. It's really my
mother speaking to me, teaching me.

"Frrreckles!" I shout, and point to the little dots on my
face.

"Frrreckles!" the students call back.

I sigh. "That was pretty good," I say.

"Yes, it was," Mom says. "That's my girl!" She beams
proudly.

I step away from the doorway to the middle of the
room. My finger trembles while I point. "Nnnnose," I say.

"Nnnnose," they repeat.

I take off my sandal and wiggle my foot. "Ttttoes,"
I say.

"Ttttoes."

"You've got it! You've got it!" Mom says. She leans against
the classroom wall to watch.

After five minutes, I've burned through everything
from *fingernail* to *eyelash* to *tooth*. By the time Mr. Special
Kingsley returns with the chair from his office, my mother's
gone. "I shall sit on the side here and complete my work
while you teach," he says. "If you require help, please
do ask."

If I require help? I pace back and forth, trying to figure
out what else I can possibly do with the students. I teach
the words *knuckle, nostril,* and *armpit* before Mr. Special
Kingsley finally looks up. His cracked glasses are halfway
down his nose. "Perhaps you might teach the children a
game. An American game," he suggests.

I swallow and glance at my backpack on the floor. I've
got nothing against common sense, but right now, it

doesn't help. My mind is blank. Game. Game. I can't think of one, so I wiggle my nose and chant in my mind:

Hocus-pocus full of fear,

Make forty more Bingo cards instantly appear.

No luck.

"What do the children in your country do for fun?" Mr. Special Kingsley asks.

"Fun?" I say, as if it's a word in a foreign language.

The truth is it's been a really long time since I had fun back home. Last May, the day after Mom's heart attack, instead of meeting Marcella and Sydni at Jamaica Pond, I lay in my bed, stared at the ceiling, and thought about how incredibly far it was from the floor. In July, for my thirteenth birthday, Dad took Marcella and me to a fancy restaurant at the top of the Prudential Center, but instead of admiring the sunset while eating cake, I sat in the restaurant bathroom and cried as Marcella pounded on the door. When October came, I should have been painting a picture of fiery leaves that littered our front lawn. But instead, I sat on the front steps without my jacket and felt the windy chill burn my cheeks raw. And when the holidays finally crashed into our lives in December, I didn't trudge through Coolidge Corner with Dad to get hot chocolate as the snow fell. Instead, I walked on the icy sidewalks by myself and thought about how my father and I hadn't watched a single vintage superhero episode together since our lives had turned upside down.

"I mean, the children in the United States of America. What do they do to enjoy themselves?" Mr. Special Kingsley asks.

Think. Think! I order myself. *Fun. Fun. Fun.* I grab on to my pendant and stick my teeth into the groove.

"*What about Simon Says?*" Mom suggests. "*You always liked that when you were in kindergarten, Clare.*"

"Zikomo," *I whisper.*

Mom looks puzzled.

"*It means* 'thanks'," *I say.*

I tell Mr. Special Kingsley that Simon Says is a fun game lots of kids in my country like to play.

"Very well, Clare," Mr. Special Kingsley says. "But I must ask you, who is Simon and what does he say?"

"I'm not really sure exactly who he is, but he tells you what to do. It's the name of the game—Simon Says."

"Ahh," Mr. Special Kingsley says. "A game called Simon. *Chonde!* Teach the children Simon."

I explain the directions: "Do what I say, not what I do. And only if Simon says it first." Mr. Special Kingsley translates into Chichewa.

But when a boy in the middle of the room tries to touch his toes, he sends half of the class tumbling over like dominoes. And everyone is copying what I'm doing instead of doing what I'm saying. Plus, there are so many kids in the room that it's impossible to see when someone is out. And I'm really sweating.

Mental note: Teachers need double deodorant.

The game is a disaster, but half an hour later, with Mr. Special Kingsley's help, we're singing the song "Head, Shoulders, Knees, and Toes" in a four-part round. And honestly, it sounds amazing!

The students sing it twice through before Mr. Special

Kingsley tells me he will now teach the standard one math lesson. "A fine beginning, Clare," he says. "You have planted a hundred seventy-six flowers this morning."

"A hundred seventy-six!" I exclaim. I'm shocked. My hand will fall off if I even try to make enough Bingo cards for the students to work in pairs.

"That is the number enrolled in this classroom. Of course, they are not all here every day. Students come from many villages throughout Machinga district. Attendance depends on the rains, the sickness, the harvest. I shall see you back tomorrow," he says. "I do give thanks for your tremendous and most illuminating service."

"You're welcome, sir," I say, and turn to head back to the standard eight classroom. But I'm not even through the doorway when I spin back around.

"Here," I say to Mr. Special Kingsley. I hand him the stack of Bingo cards. "You might need this paper to write some important letters."

Mr. Special Kingsley turns the cards over and looks through my designs while the standard one students stare at us both with great curiosity.

"Ahhh!" he says, and pushes his glasses up his nose to get a better look. "Magnificent! I . . . I . . . I do not have words for this marvelous gift you make for your headmaster. *Zikomo kwambiri!*"

I gasp. My headmaster just broke his own rule! Only the smallest children in the school are allowed to speak Chichewa. Everyone knows that.

"I do apologize," he says. "It is just that the beauty of your gift sent me back to the native tongue. Please do not tell my secret to the older students," he says, and smiles.

"Yes, sir," I say. "I mean, no, sir. I mean, yes, sir, I won't tell, sir." I'm all mixed up and I've taught my class and now I really need to go.

As I hike across the field to the standard eight classroom, I remind myself that Mr. Special Kingsley said I was tremendous and illuminating, but I'm still trembling like I survived an encounter with a wild beast.

That doesn't really happen, though, until an hour later.

CHAPTER 20

Mrs. Tomasi is wrapped in green and purple cloths, looking very much like an eggplant while she talks to everyone under the blue gum tree. I flop onto the ground beside Memory, feeling soggy and listless from my first day on the job. Mrs. Tomasi's explaining that we're going to build things called anemometers.

"What?" I whisper.

"Anemometers," Memory whispers back. "To measure wind."

After Mrs. Tomasi finishes giving the instructions, we all traipse toward the bush in search of our materials: bamboo, sticks, and calabash. "What about the leopard?" I ask, pausing at the edge of the thicket.

"That was long time ago," Memory says. "Leopards move quick. No new reports. It is certainly gone." She pushes aside a tangle of vines and steps into the forest. A second later, I hear a noise.

I jump. "What is it?" I ask.

"What is what?" Memory says.

"That noise."

"There is no noise," she says. "Only noise in the mind. Now do tell me"—she grabs a bamboo stalk—"how is the teacher?" She tries to snap the stalk in half, but it's too thick to break. "Saidi! Saidi!" she calls.

A second later he thrashes through the bramble. Memory points to the bamboo, and Saidi fishes a small knife out of his pants pocket while she tells him, "This girl teach school today."

It hits me: I actually did. I taught school. I really am a teacher!

"We must take the teacher to the lake."

"Awesome!" I say. "I mean, *yaboo!*"

Agnes pops through the branches of the bush behind us. *"Yaboo?"* she asks. "What is *yaboo?*"

Saidi saws the bamboo stalk with his knife. "What is awesome," he tells Agnes, "is that Memory, Innocent, and myself—the one, the only Saidi Tembo—shall take our new American friend to Lake Malombe this weekend."

"I do love the lake!" Agnes says. She jumps over the plant leaves into the clearing, looks up at Saidi, and bats her eyelashes. "Should you desire my company, I shall be obliged to attend."

Memory answers for him. For us. "No!" she says. On that note, the bamboo stalk cracks and we all jump out of the way.

Saidi picks up one end of the pole and drags it toward the blue gum tree. Agnes follows close behind.

Memory and I venture deeper into the bush to search for calabash. We walk for more than ten minutes through dappled green leaves and scarlet wildflowers. We arrive at a river, and Memory points to a patch of swollen green squash that hangs from a vine by the bank. I push through the thicket and place both my hands on a gourd. It feels hot, like a chunk of sun has fallen right inside of it.

But how can a calabash measure the wind? I'm about to ask Memory this when I hear someone trumpet. I glance down the river and gasp: It shimmers, silver in the sunlight. It dunks under the water. When it comes up, its huge ears slap drops of elephant water onto the river. The sun catches its eye and turns it ruby red.

"*Tibwerere*," Memory says quietly. "Let us return."

But I don't move. Can't move. The incredible creature bends its leathery trunk in a loop. An instant later, a smell more foul than dead fish fills the air. The elephant, still luxuriating in her bath, doesn't seem to notice.

Memory pinches her nostrils with one hand. With the other, she grabs my wrist and pulls me into the bush. "Gas of the elephant," she says.

"Ewww!" I shriek.

Once we can't see the river anymore, Memory stops to rest. We're both huffing and puffing. "Never get this close to elephant," she says. She waves her hand in front of her face. Clutching my side and giggling, I follow her back to the blue gum tree.

"It is a serious thing," she says, gasping.

"The gas of the elephant?" I ask.

"No," Memory says. "Elephant . . ." She lifts her flip-flop and stomps it onto the ground like she's killing a bug. "Mother elephant do that . . . on person who go close to the baby. We do not see baby elephant, so we do not know if we are close or far."

"Oh," I say. It's not funny, but I can't stop laughing until Mrs. Tomasi orders us to begin building our anemometers. First, we cut our calabashes in half with the knives Saidi and Norman keep in their pockets. Next, we scoop the warm, squishy pulp out with our bare hands. The pulp sticks in our fingernails, turning them an orangey, burnt sienna color. After that, we take two sticks and attach one empty half to each of the four ends. Then, finally, we hammer our bamboo pole into the ground with a large rock so it's standing straight up.

"Now I shall demonstrate," Mrs. Tomasi says. She picks up our sticks and crosses them at the center. Norman gives her one of the nails he's carved out of bamboo with his pocketknife. Mrs. Tomasi holds the crossed sticks at the top of the bamboo pole. "Clare, please do hammer the nail into place," she says. But I can't reach the top of the pole, so Norman goes into the classroom and carries a bench outside for me to stand on.

No sooner do I pound in the nail with a rock than the wind blows, our anemometer spins, and an incredible feeling pinwheels through my chest.

CHAPTER 21

After school, I tell Mrs. Bwanali about my first day of teaching, and during dinner, I tell Dad. "Not only do you look like your mother," he says, and smiles, "but now you're acting like her too." Dad says we should go to the trading center and get a candy bar at the Slow but Sure Shop to celebrate.

"Sounds good to me!" I say, because everyone knows there's no happy occasion complete without some chocolate. And what better way to help the chocolate go down than a nice bottle of grape Fanta?

Dad and I stand together outside the shop. "Your mother would kill me for giving you so much sugar," he says. He presses his fingers into the corners of his eyes and shakes his head.

"What's wrong, Dad?" I ask. But I know what's wrong. I raise my glass bottle. "To the future. To adventures. To our family," I say, because even though Mom isn't right here with us at the Slow but Sure Shop, who's to say she's not somewhere nearby? And even though it's only Dad and me, maybe two people can be enough for a family after all.

Dad presses his lips together. "To our family," he says softly, and we clink our bottles together and guzzle them down.

The grape soda is delicious, but I should have predicted I'd need the bathroom seconds after I finish it. Still, why use the pit latrine behind the shops when we've got a perfectly good marble seat at our house? Dad and I give Mr. Khumala, the shopkeeper, our empty bottles and get back in the Land Rover.

As if it isn't strange enough to live in a country where big monkeys walk the roads and girls press their dresses with hot rocks, things turn even weirder tonight as we're riding back from town.

"Now, tell me," Dad says as he navigates the bumpy road, "what about that project for Mrs. Middleton?"

I don't say anything.

"We've been here two and a half weeks."

"Yeah, yeah. I know."

"Better get started, kiddo," he says. "Mrs. Middleton's going to want to see something of quality."

I can only grunt, because I've already tried to write a report and a rap, but it's impossible to find the words to explain what it's like to drive through Kenmore Square to the airport one day and land on what feels like a whole other planet the next.

Dad hasn't even pulled all the way into the gravel driveway, but I open the door of the Land Rover anyway. I need to get away from this conversation almost as much as I need to go to the bathroom. I run in the dark through the yard, and I'm almost at the front door when something slithers around my ankle.

"Ahhh!" I shriek.

"What? What?" Dad comes running.

I'm dizzy with fear. "Ma . . . mamba!" I shout. I feel the deadly snake on my ankle. I try not to do my business right on its head. That might only make things worse.

"Stay calm," Dad says. "Walk . . . slowly . . . to the . . ." His voice fades into the background. I step backward. The vicious reptile's not letting go.

"Stay still," Dad whispers.

"Can't!" I croak. I shake my leg furiously to get the hideous cold-blooded hose full of poison off me, when suddenly there's a noise.

"Huh?" Dad says.

We hear it again.

"Huh?" I say.

For the third time, Dad and I hear the sound: not a venomous hiss but a seriously annoyed cluck.

We look down, and as our eyes adjust to the dark, we see the offender: a chicken! His beady eyes twinkle in the moonlight. His leg is tied to a rope—a rope that feels just like a snake.

"What're you doing here?" I shriek. "You scared me to death, you stupid thing!"

"You really think it understands English, Clare?"

I shrug. "I don't know. Do you think he speaks Chicken?"

"Possibly Chicken," Dad says. "Or Chichewa." He unties the end of the rope from the door handle. "Well, that was a close call," he says. I turn in circles as Dad untangles my leg from the rope. Then he walks the chicken into the house like it's a pet dog on a leash.

When Dad flicks the switch, the fluorescent lights buzz. The chicken flaps its wings like mad while I run past him to the bathroom.

By the time I get back to the living room, the chicken has managed to fly onto the brown couch.

"Now, who in the world would leave us a chicken?" I ask, finally chilling out a bit.

Dad hands me the end of the chicken leash. "Must be some type of gift," he says, and pads away into the kitchen.

I tie one end of the rope to the leg of the coffee table.

"So, what do you think, Clare?" Dad says as he clangs around with the pots and pans. "Sweet and sour? Fried? Betcha Mrs. Bwanali can fix up something terrific tomorrow."

Well, our new chicken may not speak English, but for sure he understands it. He flies around the sofa frantically. Then he stops cold turkey, cocks his head to the side, and stares straight into my eyes. There's no doubt about it: this chicken is begging for his life!

Dad marches back into the living room, an enormous knife in his hand. "Okay," he says. "I'll take it out back."

I freeze.

"Gimme the rope, Clare."

I untie the rope from the leg of the coffee table *reeeaaal sloooow* to give me enough time to think. I need to think.

Think about what to do. But then the rope is untied and there's no time left to think. Only to act boldly and swiftly, like Wonder Woman confronting the Legion of Doom.

I scoop the poor piece of poultry off the sofa, sprint to my bedroom, and slam the door. I lean against it while the chicken breathes heavily in my hands. In. Out. In. Out. His heart pounds triple-time. *Ba-boom. Ba-boom. Ba-boom.* The beat of my own heart marches along with his.

"Clare," Dad calls through the door. "Open up."

I tell myself not to show fear. Superheroes never do. It's part of what helps them psych out the enemy. I take a breath, get a grip. "We will *not* eat Fred," I state firmly.

"Fred?" Dad asks.

My room glows. Through the window screen, I see stars. Not just one, but a million. And all of a sudden, I know that this country does strange stuff to people. It's made Dad a little more normal. It's made me rescue a chicken.

"Yes, Fred!" I shout. I never planned this fate, but now here I am, Chicken Rescue Girl. I look at Fred. His brown feathers are silky soft. His life is literally in my hands.

Before I begin negotiations, I close my eyes and wish on a star that Fred will have a long and happy life. "Repeat after me," I say.

My father doesn't answer.

"I will never touch a feather on this chicken's head," I say louder, in case he's having trouble hearing through the door. While I wait for Dad to give his solemn oath to respect Fred's life, I look into Fred's beady eyes. He looks like a scared little baby, even though I'm pretty sure he's all grown up.

Fred clucks.

I rub my cheek against his feathers.

Fred squawks.

"Sorry," I whisper. "For a second I was thinking you were a dog or something. But listen up, Fred." His little head cocks to the side. "I won't leave you. Ever!" I tell him.

I hear Dad sigh. It's one of those loud, exaggerated sighs that means your opponent is finally giving up. "We did it," I whisper to Fred.

Right on cue, Dad says, "Okay, okay. I won't kill it. Promise. We'll keep it around as a . . . a . . ."

For all of Dad's faults, one thing he doesn't do is lie, so I fearlessly set Fred down and open the bedroom door. "Say hello to our new pet chicken!" I say.

"*Moni,*" Dad mumbles before he goes into the kitchen and heats up the *nsima, ndiwo,* and beans that Mrs. Bwanali left on the stove for our dinner again. Meanwhile, Chicken Rescue Girl, aka me, walks Fred around the house to give him a little exercise. We prance right past Dad to the screened-in veranda, where the sound of crickets and bullfrogs is so loud that it's insane.

"You can sleep here in the fresh air," I tell Fred. He flies onto the puffy green chair. "Try not to scratch up the furniture."

It's completely obvious: Fred feels right at home. Maybe too much at home. "You cannot make chicken poop on the chair!" I say.

Dad peeks into the veranda from the kitchen. "I sure hope you're not expecting Fred to make lizard poop," he says.

"Very funny," I say, and he tosses me a rag.

After I clean up the poop, I wash my hands three times with soap. Then I get the empty cardboard box Dad used to pack his medical books for the trip here. By the time I get back to the veranda, though, Fred has done it again.

I point to the poop. Fred cocks his head to the side and blinks guiltily.

"Smelly!" Dad says, and tosses me another rag.

Fred and I exchange a worried look. We both know his life is on the line. "You need to get yourself potty-trained ASAP if you know what's good for you," I whisper. Then I lift my feathered friend and put him down inside the box. "Your very own pit latrine," I say. "From now on, you need to do it here."

In the morning, I've just put on my school uniform when I get an idea: I tie my bright purple scarf with blue stars around my waist. After all, if I'm going to be a teacher, I can't wear the exact same uniform as all my students.

Once I'm dressed, I check on Fred. That's when I get a big surprise: an egg is lying in the corner of the green chair. It's a perfect, tan-colored oval egg, exactly like you'd see on a TV commercial. I reach over and pick it up. It's still warm. "Wow, Fred!" I say. "You're a girl!"

Fred clucks.

I peek in the box. Fred did good! "Nice work," I tell her. Then I take the egg to the kitchen, where Mrs. Bwanali is cleaning the counters and Dad is sitting at the table reading and shoveling toast into his mouth. I hold out my hand to show him the egg. "Glad you didn't slice and dice her?" I ask.

"Mmmm," he says, and closes the medical book he's reading.

Of course, Mrs. Bwanali is more impressed by the finer things in life. "A more beautiful dress," she says, spinning me around to check out my accessory. "Now not another second! Show Mrs. Bwanali the egg."

I hold it up for her to examine.

She throws the rag onto her shoulder, takes the egg out of my hand, and turns it around as if it is also a girl in a dress. "This egg is a beautiful egg. A beautiful egg that shines. It is an egg like a queen. If this egg is a person, this egg dress in fine clothes. This egg have shoes."

I don't know what to say, but then again, even if I did, I wouldn't have a prayer of getting a word in edgewise with all the yolky compliments Mrs. Bwanali is frying up. "You may eat this egg for breakfast or give this egg to a school friend," she says. "Remember, Clare, always keep your hen warm."

"Her name is Fred."

"Fred," Mrs. Bwanali says. "I like this American name. This hen, Fred, may like to sleep under the bed, you know. The temperature is good there." Mrs. Bwanali is full of advice about how to get Fred to produce enough eggs to share with Memory, Innocent, Saidi, Patuma, and Winnie. "Talk to Fred. Tell her what you do, what you like. Ask Fred question about her day. A happy hen is a prize more great than gold!"

I sit down at the table and Mrs. Bwanali serves me

white tea, toast with jam, and the freshest, most delicious egg I've ever tasted while I guess who the chicken is from. "I think it's from you!" I say.

Mrs. Bwanali is tickled. "My girl, Clare, think Mrs. Bwanali is a queen," she tells Dad. "She think Mrs. Bwanali have chicken to give here and chicken to give there." This really cracks her up. "I tell you what, my girl," she says. "If I do get a chicken to keep, I give it to Fred. Then Fred have chicken friend. Everyone need a friend. Even a chicken."

CHAPTER 22

During morning assembly, as I sing along to the national anthem, students from other classes whisper about my new dress. I feel like I've walked right out of one of those fashion magazines Marcella reads all the time.

After assembly, I cross the field to the standard one room, throw back my shoulders, and step inside. I position myself center stage and wait for my audience to file in and take their seats on the floor. With my new and improved uniform, I definitely feel more like a teacher than yesterday. I clear my throat. "Good morning!" I say, and 176 students reply, "Good morning, madam."

We play a few rounds of Simon Says before I teach them the hokey-pokey. Soon they are wiggling their rear ends and laughing up a storm. Mr. Special Kingsley has to clear his throat three times before order is restored. At the end of the hour, my headmaster says, "Tomorrow it shall be time to introduce the students to the English alphabet."

And I know the jig is up. Sure, I can play games with kids, but real teaching is going to be a whole different story.

As soon as I meet up with Innocent and Memory on the hilltop after school, I blurt out my question. "Okay, call me stupid," I say, "but how're you supposed to teach without any teaching materials?"

Memory knits her eyebrows together. "Without materials?" she says.

"You know what I mean—pencils, paper, chalk, chalkboards, even markers, and posters with the letters of the alphabet on them that hang all around the classroom. Colored paper, glue, scissors. Flashcards with math facts. Maps of the world. Teaching materials to help kids learn."

Innocent waits for us to get moving, his hand on his little hip.

"There is plenty," Memory says.

I glance at the bookmobile. The bookmobile, which contains all fifty-three books for our entire school. "No, no, I really don't think so," I say.

"Tatiye," Memory tells Innocent. She points the bookmobile down the hill and marches straight back to the school building.

"Where are you going?" I ask, following behind.

Memory doesn't answer, but a mysterious grin creeps across her face. She walks through the schoolyard to the standard one classroom, parks the bookmobile inside it, and leads me through a thicket of acacia trees to a field.

A tower rises from the ground like a smokestack.

"What is this?" I ask, stunned by the odd sight.

"Mud," she says. "Home to termite bug." I glance across the field. Hundreds of termite hills rise against the yellow ochre sky.

"Wow! Those have to be ten feet tall! Big houses for little bugs."

After Memory tells Innocent something in Chichewa, he ambles over to the closest tower, reaches his arms out straight in front of him, and digs his fingers into the mud. A bunch of critters fly out as Innocent pulls off three hunks of clay and gives them to his sister.

Memory squats on the ground and rolls two long lines and a short one. She pinches the long lines together at the top and sticks the short line across them in the middle. "Letter A," she says. "Bake in sun to make hard. What do I tell you? Plenty of teaching material."

Sure, my students can each have a letter, but how will they scribble and doodle and daydream? Isn't that what childhood is all about?

But it's like Memory can read my mind. She picks up a stick and writes the letter A in the dirt. I give up.

"I see," I say with a sigh. "There is plenty."

Memory, Innocent, and I are passing the tea farm.

"What are you looking at?" I ask.

"Sky," Memory says.

As I push the bookmobile, Innocent shows me a few

karate moves. Wouldn't you know it, his uncle Stallard saw a Jackie Chan movie in Blantyre last week and told him all about it. Now Innocent is convinced that one day he'll break boards with his bare hands. He shows me a sideways kick. "Awesome!" I say.

Memory's still got her eyes pinned on the clouds, so I reach up and feel my hair. "You think it's going to rain?" I ask. My hair always knows the weather first, but the outer layer doesn't feel rough and frizzy, so if it does rain, I doubt it will be a full-on storm.

"I search for the airplane," she says. "Uncle Stallard tell me this is how you and your father travel to our country. He tell me about the girls on the airplane who serve the Coca-Colas. He say one day Innocent shall be a karate master, but I shall be air hostess. When I am the air hostess, I shall take airplane to your country. I shall come to school and watch you teach."

Suddenly, I'm confused. Not only about the airplane, but also about my dream. "I was going to be an artist who paints sets for plays," I say. "But that was before I became a teacher. Now I'm not so sure. I mean, I do love working with my school theater back home, although I did skip out on painting the sets for *Grease*, but that was only because . . . well, it's a long story."

By the time I shut my trap, Memory's staring at me like I've got a calabash growing right out of my nose, so I back up a hundred yards. "Well, you know what a play is, right?"

"A play?" Memory asks.

"With actors who tell a story."

"*Inde*," she says. "Sometimes I act out stories behind the hut with my cousins." She confers with Innocent in

Chichewa and then says, "Innocent say he hope you shall be star of the play."

"Oh, no, no, no. Not me!" I say, although lately I've been thinking I might want to give that a try someday. "For right now, I design costumes and paint sets." When I finish my explanation, Memory has a mischievous glint in her eyes. "What is it?" I ask.

"You see that boy?" She juts her chin toward her brother.

"Of course I see him," I say.

"Are you the teacher of this boy?"

Why do I have the distinct feeling I'm being led into some sort of trap? "Yeeesss," I say, slow and unsure.

"A good teacher shall use all her godly gifts to teach, correct?" She maneuvers the bookmobile around a puddle.

"Yeeesss."

Memory and Innocent talk for a good long time in Chichewa. Before I know it, he's grinning from ear to ear and doing karate chops at the air. "My brother agree. He shall be actor in the show."

Innocent smiles, those dimples pucker, and before I know it, the three of us are back at my house sitting on the veranda, planning a play to help the standard one students learn more English—a play starring Innocent Matinga! Of course, I have to clean up Fred's poop first, because even though Mrs. Bwanali and I have trained her to go in the box by rewarding her with bits of banana, sometimes she has a rather smelly accident.

"There is no better way to learn," Memory insists as she bounces on the puffy green chair in the veranda, and we all watch Fred prance across the floor.

"The actors can perform for the whole school," I chime in.

"Brilliant!" Memory says as Innocent strokes Fred's wattle.

After Mrs. Bwanali serves us orange juice and delicious *mbatata* biscuits, we get down to the business of writing the script. "What do you think our play should be about?" I ask.

"*Nkhuku*," Innocent tells Memory, who tells me.

"A chicken? Why a chicken?" I ask.

Memory laughs. "This boy love *nkhuku*! For a whole month, he try to catch *nkhuku* for dinner. The month before this month, he finally succeed. The chicken was boy chicken, so Grandmother let him eat chicken feet."

Fred flaps her wings.

"Shhh!" I whisper. "I don't want Fred to get nervous."

Even though Memory and Innocent think I should consider eating Fred, they are happy to leave with the egg Fred laid today. But they are useless in helping me solve the mystery: who in the world left this happy hen at my door?

The next morning after assembly, Memory and I catch Mr. Special Kingsley before he disappears into his office. Memory is so excited that she forgets to speak English while she tells our headmaster all about the play. I'm sure he's going to say we should forget it. I could swear he's going to say that a real teacher would never come up with a cockamamie idea like this.

Instead he asks, "Did you designate a part for every student?"

Memory looks at me and I look at her. Our play has only five roles. But before we can explain this to Mr. Special Kingsley, he says, "Magnificent! Every student in standard one shall act in the show. I shall consult the *sing'anga* to find out the best evening, the one with the full moon."

"Sir, there are a hundred seventy-six students in standard one," I say.

"Yes, it is wonderful. All the families shall watch the show on best evening."

"Best evening, sir?" I ask. "Best evening for what?"

"For the play," Memory says, and sighs.

"The village chiefs shall invite all the villagers," Mr. Special Kingsley explains. "It will be an evening of delight for everyone and it shall show mothers and fathers the value of educating their children here at our school."

"Sir, we can perform the show for the standard two class," I say. "I promise you, sir, that audience will be plenty big for us."

But Mr. Special Kingsley has a dream of his own, and it seems that now he can't be swayed. "I anticipate perhaps a thousand visitors to our school for this show. We shall need torches to ward off the snakes."

I gulp.

"You are late for class, girls. Hurry along. And Memory, it is English. Always English for students in the senior standards. I do not fancy to hear you speaking Chichewa again when you are at school."

With that, Mr. Special Kingsley pushes his glasses higher on his nose and limps through the doorway into the office.

"It's impossible," I whisper to Memory once he's out of sight. "There's no way we can have parts for all the standard one students!"

Memory doesn't respond. Instead, she marches straight across the field to the standard one classroom. I lug my down-and-out soul across the schoolyard after her. By the time I arrive, 176 children are giggling, gasping, and screeching like they've just been cast on Broadway.

CHAPTER 23

Mr. Special Kingsley and Mrs. Tomasi have agreed to let Memory work with me in the standard one classroom for the first thirty minutes of class each morning in order to help the students prepare for the show.

Of course, since Memory's going to teach like me, she can't wear a plain old school uniform anymore, so yesterday after we dropped the books off in the trading center, we went back to my house and I let her pick one of my scarves to tie around her waist. She chose the orange one with gold threads woven through it. I untied it from the band of scarves on my dresser.

"It is like sunshine," Memory said as I tied the scarf around her waist. "I do feel like the teacher now." Then she thanked me for the gift.

This morning, all the girls in our class complimented

Memory's new belt—all except for Agnes, who said it's even more *kunyasa*—ugly—than mine.

It's hard to believe, but we've actually got worse problems than Agnes. The witch doctor said the ninth night of March would have the most moonlight, so now we've got the jitters. And yesterday, Mr. Special Kingsley told us that he invited the chiefs to bring the villagers from all the surrounding villages.

Now Memory and I have added 171 roles to the original script, so every standard one student is a member of the cast. There are fifty hippos, fifty hyenas, and fifty hunters. Plus, twenty-five kids will play the howling wind in the storm scene. And then, of course, there is the *nkhuku*, performed by Innocent. Our actors will speak in English, and Memory will translate into Chichewa for all the parents and other villagers in the audience, since many of them haven't gone to school and don't speak much English at all.

The good thing is that between listening to Memory translate and studying my vocabulary words from Mrs. Tomasi, I've picked up enough Chichewa that when Saidi says it's time to plan our trip to Lake Malombe, I can tell him, *"Nkhani yabwino! Ndakufunitsitsa kunyanja!"* In other words, "Wonderful! I can't wait to relax at the lake!"

Saidi told me he's been saving his money from selling reeds on the weekends for a surprise he'll give to us during our outing. Memory and I are all about trying to guess what he's got planned. "There is a restaurant at the lake. Perhaps he shall purchase an ice cream sundae," she whispers to me.

Today I'm coughing and sneezing like mad. "Saidi will

get an ice cream sundae for each of us," I suggest, and pray that these allergies don't get the best of me before we set out for our road trip. I kick my backpack to the side of our table. Memory hands it over, and I pull out a packet of tissues I brought all the way from the good old U. S. of A.

By Saturday morning, the allergy medicine is working and I feel a lot better. My nose is hardly running anymore. I grab my Red Sox cap. "And don't forget to put on the sunscreen," Dad says as we bump down the narrow path to the main road.

"As if!" I tell him. With fair skin like mine, I'm not about to forget. Even with daily sunscreen, my skin has turned a reddish cinnamon hue.

"And make sure you're back by dark," Dad says. "I'll be home from work by then."

"Okay," I say.

Dad turns on the main road. "Been meaning to ask you, how are the practice tests going?" In addition to the horrible assignment, Mrs. Middleton also gave me a pile of MCAS practice tests.

"Clare," she had said, "I'm letting you do this because I know you're a smart girl. There are plenty of students who are homeschooled, and you are going to be homeschooling yourself. Now learn a lot and have a wonderful experience. I know it will do you good to get away."

Even though Dad thinks MCAS stands for Massachusetts Comprehensive Assessment System, I know that it really means Most Clueless Arrangement of Stuff you could ever think to ask anybody ever! They list problems like:

The total area of Massachusetts is 10,555 square miles, including bodies of water. If 1 square mile is 2.58998 square kilometers, approximately how many square kilometers is Massachusetts?

A. 17,000
B. 20,500
C. 27,000
D. 36,500

But they never list the real answer: E. Who cares!

Still, I tell Dad that the studying is going fine, because I don't want him to ask for evidence. I've only taken two practice tests this whole time. I can't bear to do another one.

Speaking of things I can't stand, when Dad pulls over at the kiosk near the Slow but Sure Shop, I glare through the windshield at the party crasher. I sure as heck hope she isn't the surprise Saidi has planned! Agnes stands on the edge of the dirt road, her arm threaded through his.

Dad opens his wallet. "Here's a few thousand *kwacha*. Should be more than enough to help you and your friends get to the lake." He hands me the bills, which I tuck into my backpack before I slide out of the Land Rover with a big fake smile on my face.

"*Moni!*" I call like everything's cool.

"*Moni,*" everyone says, and waves.

Agnes turns to Saidi. "It shall be lovely to feel the sunshine at the beach today," she says.

I definitely don't want to stand near her, so I go into

the Slow but Sure Shop and buy a bottle of water for each of us.

While we wait at the minibus stop, we guzzle our bottles of water. "I never did drink the expensive water in the bottle," Memory says.

"I did," Agnes calls over to us. "When my auntie visits from Lilongwe she always buys me the water in the bottle. I did drink it already three times in my life."

I swallow. I wonder what Marcella would do if she was here. Would she be amused by Agnes and all her drama? Maybe, but I'm not, so I hang around with Innocent and Memory instead.

I've already taught the standard one class to count to ten in English, so I figure Innocent's ready to learn one of my favorite childhood games. "I one the cake," I say. "Now you say, 'I two the cake.'"

"I two the cake," Innocent says, and giggles.

"I three the cake," I say.

"I four the cake." He catches on.

But after he says "I eight the cake," he doesn't laugh.

"Get it? You *ate* the cake!" I say.

He stares at me blankly with his enormous brown eyes, so I have to spend the next five minutes explaining why it's funny while Memory translates. After that, we play all over again. This time Innocent laughs. *Hello, Dimples!*

By the time the minibus arrives, we've finished our water. The driver opens the back door and I dole out enough money for us all. Even though Saidi offered to pay for Memory and Innocent, I let him know that my father insists he save his money. There's a smelly goat standing in the aisle. Innocent plops down on his sister's lap, and I squeeze between the two of them and the window.

Once we're all settled, the driver moseys into the Slow but Sure Shop. It isn't long until he returns with three sacks of maize. He shoves one under my feet and one under Memory's feet. Then he plops one bag onto my lap without even asking if it's okay. I want to throw it on the floor but it weighs a ton, and there isn't room for it anyway.

Somehow I manage to turn my head to glance at Saidi, who's stuck in back beside Agnes. "Poor thing," I say. Memory turns to take a look for herself.

"Poor boy!" she agrees.

The driver starts the engine, and I take another quick peek. That's when I notice something strange: Saidi's got a big fat grin across his face. "Look!" I tell Memory. After she does, we both gag out loud. We can't decide which is making us sicker: seeing Saidi so happy, or the smell of the goat mixed with the heat and the bumps.

I think about asking Memory all my questions: about whether she carries a bucket of tears inside her heart, and whether the bucket gets lighter or heavier as the years pass. I want to tell her about my mother, but I don't really know how to begin. Instead, as we wind through Machinga, Memory and I make Innocent practice his lines for the play, but our leading man falls asleep right at the start of our rehearsal. So, for more than an hour as we bump along, Memory and I discuss the casting, the costumes, and the set.

At last, I spy a thin line of turquoise out the window. The line gradually expands to a glimmering, sparkling lake that's so big it looks like an ocean. Two moped drivers whiz by. Memory nudges Innocent awake. "I ate the cake," he mumbles before he opens his eyes. Memory and I crack up.

The second I step out of the minibus, a warm breeze blows through my hair. I inhale the clean, fresh air. Restaurants built on stilts dot the side of the beach, and sunbathers relax under the palm trees on the warm gray sand.

We walk down to the beach, where I unbuckle my sandals. It sure does feel super to squish the sand through my toes. I spread out my towel under a palm tree and take off my shirt and skirt. "Want to go swimming now?" I ask.

That's when I notice Agnes and Memory staring at me, and Saidi looking out at the water for a long, long time. "It is interesting, this purple uniform, with your bare skin for all boys to see," Agnes says.

In an instant, I feel sunburned all over, like I don't even have a bathing suit on. No wonder Saidi is staring at the lake. He's embarrassed! Even though Agnes has had several bottles of storebought water in her life, apparently this is her first trip to the lake. I must be the first person she's ever seen up close in a bathing suit. I'm mortified! I grab my shirt and pull it over my head. I put my skirt back on as fast as I can while Memory says, "It is interesting this swim clothing. All the tourist have this, Agnes."

Agnes looks around and I do too. Memory's right. There are lots of people on the beach in their bathing suits, but I won't be one of them. I don't want to be a tourist. I guess my friends were planning to swim in their clothes.

"I think Innocent need some water," Memory says. He's fallen back to sleep in her arms.

"*Malawi kwacha*," Agnes says, and holds out her palm. "I shall do the job. I shall fetch the clean drinking water for my friends."

Saidi is obviously saving his money for something else, so I reach into my backpack and pull out a few bills. I give them to Agnes just so she'll leave me alone. She takes the money and walks over to the Chomp and Chew Stop while Memory sits on the sand, rocks Innocent, and sings to him like she's his mother.

I stretch out on the towel and let the sun wrap me in its rays. I close my eyes and think about how good the last few weeks have turned out. I've already made friends, and I'm happier than I've been in a long time.

Ten minutes later, though, the sand castle of good feelings I'm building crumbles. My lips are parched. My tongue is dry. I need a drink, and Agnes still isn't back with our water. "Did she fall in the lake?" I ask.

Saidi decides to explore. He walks across the sand and into the Chomp and Chew Stop. When he finally comes out, we can see that he's furious. Agnes is with Saidi, but she isn't carrying any bottles. Instead, melted chocolate ice cream dribbles down her face. "I do apologize," she says, and giggles. "It looked divine. I could not refuse."

"Where's my money?" I glower.

"I do apologize," Agnes says again. "But you did not give me enough *kwacha* for water as well."

I grab my backpack and stomp across the sand to the shop, where I buy another water bottle for everyone except the crook. Memory holds one to Innocent's lips.

142

"*Imwa*, Innocent," she says. Innocent takes a couple of sips. Then we all follow Saidi down to the shade beneath the Chomp and Chew Stop.

Chained to the wooden stilts that prop up the restaurant are four wooden rowboats, each a different color. "What is your best color, Innocent?" Saidi asks as he rolls up the cuffs of his pants.

Innocent points to the green rowboat. "*Biriwira*," he says.

"You must not steal a boat," Memory tells Saidi.

Saidi puffs out his chest. "I have paid the fee inside the Chomp and Chew Stop. Remember, I am a businessman."

Saidi unwinds the rusty chain that ties the rowboat to the stilt. He must have spent a lot of his income from his weekend work on this trip, so Memory and I say, "*Zikomo kwambiri,*" which means "thanks very much," and Agnes says, "This is a man who provide."

Sand swishes under the bottom of the rowboat as he pushes it down the beach and into the water, where he holds the boat steady. Memory sets Innocent on the sand and wades in. She lifts the skirt of her *chitenje* and hoists herself into the rickety boat. I slosh in too, and set my backpack in the rowboat. The water is incredibly cool and refreshing, and I dive right in with my clothes still on. When I stand up, I wring my hair out with my hand. A bright yellow fish with orange spots circles my waist. "Look, Innocent!" I point. "A freckled fish."

Innocent doesn't come to see. He stays there on the beach, staring into the distance. Leave it to a six-year-old to do exactly the opposite of what you request.

Saidi slogs out of the lake, scoops up our little friend,

and places him on a bench inside the boat. After Saidi gets into the boat himself, he reaches over the edge to help pull me up. It's not like I mean to notice that his hand is strong and warm, but it is, and I do, and when I hold on to it, a strange wave rushes through me.

Even though I want to sit next to Saidi, I wouldn't do that to Memory, because she adores him. So I sit beside Memory and Innocent instead, and when Agnes gets in, she sits next to Saidi up front. And of course, I don't want to be jealous of Agnes, but I can't help it, I am.

Saidi picks up the two oars lying at the bottom of the boat. "I can paddle," I tell him. It's true. Our entire seventh-grade class went canoeing on Walden Pond last spring. By the end of the field trip, I wasn't half bad.

"I shall like to try," Memory says.

"You girls begin. When you are tired, then my turn." Saidi hands us the oars.

"What about Agnes?" I ask.

"I am queen. I do not row," she says. "Saidi know that."

I look to Saidi. He only shrugs like there's nothing he can do. Then he points to a cluster of brightly colored rowboats wobbling way out on the horizon. "This way to wonderful little fish," he says.

So I show Memory how to hold the oar and how to slice it into the water, but for the first ten minutes, we only manage to go backward or in circles while Agnes snickers. Once we finally get going, Agnes lifts her chin to the sun and closes her eyes. It's a good thing, because that way she doesn't notice the faces Memory and I make behind her back.

CHAPTER 24

Soon it's too hard to make faces. Memory and I are out of breath. "I need a rest," I say, glancing back at the beach. From here, the sunbathers look like dolls.

"I must rest as well," Memory says.

We hand our oars to Saidi. "The expert is here," he tells us. He's not kidding! A fierce breeze blows through my hair, and suddenly, we're cruising. And I'm staring. How can I not? Every time Saidi pulls back on the oars, the muscles in his biceps bulge.

Memory reaches over the side of the boat, scoops up some lake water, and splashes it onto her brother's forehead.

By the time Saidi decides that even the rowing expert could use a break, the beach is a strip in the distance.

Innocent sleeps while I teach Saidi, Agnes, and Memory my little game. And when Agnes says, "I eight the cake," Memory, Saidi, and I crack up, but Agnes says, "What is funny? Do not laugh."

"Number two student should understand," Memory says.

"Number one student should explain in Chichewa," Agnes replies.

So Memory explains the game in Chichewa, and when she finishes, Agnes says, "A baby game. Why must a woman such as me understand this game for babies?"

Memory and I roll our eyes. Saidi picks up the oars again, and an orange rowboat teeters into view. The people in the boat are pointing to a big rock in the shallow water near land. "What are they staring at?" I ask, when all of a sudden the rock shoots out of the water and lets out a thunderous roar. The ugly beast's mouth is big enough to swallow us in a single bite.

I'm still shrieking when it sinks under the water again. Agnes, Memory, and Saidi laugh so hard that our rowboat wobbles, which doesn't make me feel any better. Agnes wipes a tear from her cheek. "Do you like our—how do you say—*mvuu*?"

"Hip—hip—hippopotamus!" I grab on to the side of our rocking boat.

"*Mvuu*. Most dangerous animal on planet Earth," Saidi says. "Never get more near as this."

I gulp.

"It is a good thing we are still far," Saidi says. "If we are close, I will be screaming with you, Clare."

"Black mamba snake only poisons people," Agnes says. "The hippo *eats* . . ." Another rock lifts itself out of the water.

146

Memory gives Innocent a gentle rub on the belly. "Look, Innocent. *Mvuu!*" she says. Innocent doesn't move. "Innocent!" When he doesn't answer, Memory shakes him harder.

Innocent's eyes flutter. Memory's voice turns shrill and tight. She speaks to Saidi in Chichewa. A few seconds later, Saidi climbs to the front of the boat. He grunts and groans as he cuts the water with the oars.

Agnes leans her elbows against the edge of the boat and says something in Chichewa.

Memory grits her teeth.

Agnes turns to me. "All I say is, I do not see why we must ruin our day on the lake. Innocent is a tired boy. Nothing more."

I tell myself maybe Agnes is right. Maybe he's just very sleepy. But if that's true, why are the hairs on my arms stiffer than porcupine needles? Why is a haze of sweat fogging up my skin?

When we finally near the shore by the Chomp and Chew Stop, Saidi jumps into the water. He reaches into the rowboat and grabs Innocent while Memory climbs over the edge, lowering herself into the lake and soaking her skirt.

"If your desire is to worry like old hens," Agnes says, "you may. I will not wreck my excursion to the beach. A girl does need her sun and sand."

I splash over the edge of our rowboat, grab my backpack off the seat, and wade to the shore.

"You shall see," Agnes calls. "You shall see. The boy is fine. He is healthy. When you return, you shall say Agnes is a smart girl." Her voice fades into the sound of the birds and small waves as I climb onto the beach beneath the Chomp and Chew Stop.

After Saidi hands Innocent to Memory, he races across the sand toward a group of teenage boys who are playing a game of paddleball.

I tell Memory we better get Innocent to the hospital, to my dad.

Sand blows across the beach. "The distance is far," she says. "We may not have time." She presses her cheek to Innocent's forehead. "It may be malaria," she says.

My teeth chatter in the sudden chill. And I think, *Malaria? How can it be malaria? Doesn't Innocent take Malarone pills like me?*

We turn and watch the boys on the beach stop their game. The one with the long face points to a nearby hill. Saidi races into the Chomp and Chew Stop while I follow Memory up the sand to the road.

A few minutes later, Saidi bolts out of the restaurant toward us with a man who wears an orange and yellow Hawaiian shirt. The man looks at Innocent. "Cute little bloke," he says, cupping his hand on the back of Innocent's head. "I'm sure it's nothing but a little heat fatigue. If I had a *kwacha* for every kid who comes down to Lake Malombe and passes out in the sun, I'd be a rich man." The man shakes his shaved head. "Let me tell you something. You Africans need sunscreen every bit as much as us *azungu*, but as you like it. I'll drive round."

We pile into the back of the SUV, and Saidi gives directions—around the lake road, off to the right, and up a large hill. While we drive, the man chatters on about

148

the crowd in the Chomp and Chew Stop. "Best business of the year right now. Place is packed. Good times," he says, and chuckles.

When we finally reach the top of the hill, Saidi instructs the driver to turn down a craggy path. "This place," Saidi says. He points to a mountainside hut with three stalks of maize growing in the yard.

"Best of luck to you kids," the driver says. "Now off you go."

Memory gets out of the SUV with Innocent in her arms. Saidi leaves too. But I'm sure there's some mistake. This isn't where the doctor lives. "Could you wait for us?" I ask the driver. "I seriously doubt this is the right—"

"Wish I could, darlin', but like I said, loads of customers this time of year. We've rented every rowboat, every moped."

I take the bills out of my backpack and quickly count them. Four thousand Malawi *kwacha*.

"Get going now," the man says.

"Please!" I say. "I'll give you five hundred *kwacha* if you'll wait for us."

"Sorry, kid. Scoot."

I don't know what comes over me. "Okay, four thousand," I say.

The man pierces me with his stare. "Serious?"

"Dead," I say.

He looks at his watch. "Okey-dokey. Make it snappy. Name's Derek, by the—"

I don't have time to hear the rest. I jump out of the car and run across the dirt to join the others at the doorway of the hut.

Memory wipes a tear from her cheek. "The doctor," she says. "He is not here."

But a second later, a very old man with gray hair and shriveled skin appears. He looks right at me. "America?" he asks.

I nod.

He smiles a crooked smile and waves us inside the hut, where a giraffe skin is spread over the dried-mud floor. The old man instructs Memory to lay Innocent on top of it. Then he folds up an orange cloth, bends down, and slips it under Innocent's head.

The old man says something to me in Chichewa, but I don't understand. "He want ten thousand Malawi *kwacha*," Memory tells me.

"I . . . I . . . only have four thousand, but . . . but I already promised . . . I didn't think . . ."

Memory translates. The old man clicks his teeth.

Saidi takes two hundred *kwacha* out of his pocket, but obviously that isn't going to make a dent in the bill. I don't know what else to do, so I pull out everything I have, including a bunch of *tambala* coins. I drop the money into the old man's leathery hands. He closes his wrinkled fingers around the money and stuffs it into a cardboard box on a wooden table.

Beside the box are dozens of jars. The old man unscrews the cap on one and pulls out a small bone. He drops it—*clink!*—into a glass. He pours in blue liquid and stirs the mixture with a stick. Next, he crumbles up dried leaves and sprinkles them on top. Then he screws on the lid and gives the jar to Saidi.

The old man kneels on the floor by Innocent's head.

He closes his eyes, spreads his fingers wide above Innocent's face, and chants a strange melody that creeps me out. Finally, he places a large white bean on Innocent's tummy. When the bean rolls off, the old man says, "He breathe."

"He breathed before!" I cry.

"He breathe," the old man says, and nods. "Evil spirit . . ."

This man is a witch doctor. A fake! A phony!

His eyes light up. He stretches his arms out. "Gone!" he says. He hobbles over to me, taps the jar with the blue liquid, and holds up three fingers.

"Three?" I say. "*Katatu patsiku?*"

He gives me the jar and nods yes, Innocent should drink the liquid three times a day. Then he flicks his hand toward the doorway. "*Yendani bwino!*" he says, spitting out each word like a curse.

I gasp. We've been here less than five minutes, we've spent all our money, and now we're getting kicked out with nothing for Innocent but a jar of blue craziness. I whisper to Saidi that Derek's outside, and Saidi whispers to Memory. Then he bends down and lifts Innocent off the giraffe skin, and we all sprint outside to the SUV.

Memory slams the door. "*Tayendetsa!*" she shouts.

"As you like it!" Derek says.

In no time, we're racing down the hill, back to Lake Malombe.

CHAPTER 25

"**M**y father's a real doctor. He works at the Machinga District Hospital." My voice cracks. "Could you take us? Please!"

"Wish I could, my friend. But Machinga is several hours from here. See the sun? That means . . ." Derek rubs his fingers together, the international sign for money. "Got to get back to business before all the customers leave my shop. But tell you what," he says. "There's a couple inside right now that'll be heading up your way first thing in the morning. Bettin' you could hitch a ride."

"We cannot wait to sunrise," Memory says.

"Malaria," Saidi adds. "May be bad kind."

Derek looks back at us. "Listen, kids. If it was the vicious sort of malaria, that healer on the hill would've given him a fair go. Would've kept him overnight."

"That man only witch doctor!" Memory cries.

"He's a crackpot!" I shout. "He stole my money. He gave us this." I shove the jar of blue liquid toward him. Derek glances at it.

"Dunno," he says. "I've seen stranger. Could work." He sighs like he's really torn up. "Listen, I can drop you kids at the minibus stop for no extra cost. I assure you, though, the little chap will be fine. He's a bit sunbaked is all." He pulls over to the side of the road. "Now, about that four thousand," he says.

"I told you. The witch doctor took it!"

The back of Derek's neck looks like a snow cone getting filled with cherry syrup.

"I swear, I'll mail you the money. The second I get home. All four thousand—plus a tip, of course. A big tip! Or you can ask my dad for it."

"Get out of here!" Derek snarls. "All of you. Out!"

We open the SUV door and scurry away like panicked geckos.

"How can we take the minibus? We don't have enough left for even one of us to travel," I say.

"We must beg the driver for a ride," Memory says.

So we wait and wait, while Saidi holds Innocent, who is still asleep, and I pace back and forth, back and forth. I want to ask why Innocent doesn't swallow little white pills each week like I do. I want to know how it's possible that one little mosquito bite can make someone sick. But instead, I look on silently as Memory pours the drink into Innocent's lips, which are no longer pink but more of a bluish white. A man and woman on mopeds speed past us to the beach as the potion dribbles back out onto Innocent's shoulder. If we had mopeds, we wouldn't have to wait for the stupid minibus. Who even knows if the driver will take pity on us and help us out?

The tourists lock the bikes that they no doubt rented from Derek. Before they mosey down to the beach, they tuck something into the bag on the back of one of the mopeds. I think I know what it is.

Innocent's teeth chatter. His eyes are half closed, but the parts I can see are all white, and I don't need any more inspiration than that. I've never stolen anything in my life. Still, I don't think a good person would just stand around at a minibus stop and hope for the best.

CHAPTER 26

I glance at the couple, two silhouettes ankle-deep in water. "Be right back," I tell Memory and Saidi.

When I get to the mopeds, I glance around to make sure no one's looking. I slip my hand into the side pocket of the bag. I feel a couple of pens, and maybe a paper clip or two. Then I hit gold. And voilà! We've got a ride home.

I run back to Saidi and Memory with the keys to explain the plan. At first, Saidi isn't sure he can go along with it, but after Innocent lets out a moan, he agrees: we don't have another choice.

Without actually getting on the mopeds, I give Saidi and Memory a riding lesson. All those outings on mopeds with Mom during Dad's medical conferences come in handy. "It's a lot like riding your bike," I tell Saidi. "Except that it's electric." I pantomime how to flick the switch, rev the motor with the handlebar, and work the brake.

I pace the sidewalk. Too risky to take them now. The tourists are still so close. The man wraps his arm around the woman, points out at the water. That's when we all remember Agnes. There she is, a tiny dot on a green toy boat floating in the middle of the lake. "She shall at last receive her sunshine," Saidi says.

"And her exercise," I add.

Finally, the couple wades into the water and dives underneath. Now's our chance. *"Tiye tonse!"* I say.

Memory and Saidi climb onto one moped with Innocent sandwiched between them. I take the other. I wish we had helmets, but what can we do?

"Changu!" Memory says.

We turn the keys and pedal like mad. Saidi takes the lead. It's a good thing he knows the way, but it's a bad thing—a very bad thing—that he's never driven a moped before, because it wobbles and tilts to the side. The only reason he doesn't drop Innocent is that he keeps putting his feet on the ground.

But after about fifteen minutes, he catches on. We fly, then, across the miles into the last shades of day. The whole time, the red dust swirls up from the road and dances like an angry spirit under the dwindling sun. And I'm screaming inside. Screaming that my father isn't here. Screaming that I need my mother. Screaming that Innocent had better be okay.

I try to hold the edge of my T-shirt between my lips to stop the dust from going down my throat, but the wind rips it out of my mouth and screeches in my ears. I squint to keep the dust from sticking in my eyes. I can barely see

Saidi as he veers onto a smaller road. I follow him into the misty, shadowy light of dusk until the clouds crack open, the leaves shiver, and lightning flashes, bright and terrifying. "Watch out!" I yell. The words blow back in my ears, a senseless hum.

It's too late.

Saidi pounds the handlebars with his fist. I slow to a stop.

Memory wants to know what's wrong, even though it's completely obvious. The bike is stuck in a mud puddle. Well, it's obvious to Saidi and me, but not to Memory. She can't understand how something like a puddle can stop us from getting to the hospital, to my father, who can save her brother's life. But what can Saidi do? The tires are caked in mud.

Memory gets off the moped and sloshes out of the puddle with Innocent in her arms. Meanwhile, I hand Saidi the wet towel from my backpack. "The tires!" I shout over claps of thunder. "Wipe them!" Then I trudge through the mud to the edge of the road and put my hand on Innocent's leg. It's freezing, and now my towel's soaked. Why don't I have something warm and dry to wrap him in? A blanket, a coat, anything! *Is this what happens when someone dies?* I wonder. *Do dying people turn cold?*

The last time I ever saw my mother, she was in her hospital bed. I reached over and held her hand. *But was it warm or cold? Warm or cold?* I'm desperate to remember, but I can't, so instead I shout to Memory, "He'll be fine!"

A sheet of rain brushes across us like the bristles of a paintbrush. In the slate-gray light, Memory looks at me hard. "You American," she says. "Yet you do not know everything. You rich, yes," she shouts over the rain. "Therefore, you do not know."

The heavy rain washes me in a coat of gloss, sealing me in a separate world.

I search the sky.

But it isn't there.

Not a glimmer, not a sliver, not a hint of moon.

CHAPTER 27

It's dark by the time Memory grabs Innocent off the moped seat and we all run inside.

Lanterns light up the hospital waiting room. Mothers and fathers huddle on the ground, children stare at the ceiling, grandmothers rock on their heels.

A man in blue hospital scrubs steps in.

"Emergency!" I yell.

His jaw drops. When I see the gap between his front teeth, I recognize him. He's Mr. Malola, the clinical officer. I met him in Mkumba village my first time there. "Not to worry," Mr. Malola says. "The electric shut off many time in the storm." He holds a cell phone, using it like a flashlight.

"Where's my dad?" I shout. "Dr. Silver?"

"I'm sorry," he says. "Your daddy's not here." Mr. Malola glances at his clipboard. "Abdallan Sikochi."

An old man stands with a baby in his arms.

"I need my dad!" I yell. I don't feel like myself. I don't feel like anyone I ever knew. I rush to Mr. Malola. "Look!" I point at Memory and Innocent. When he sees them, I exhale. Now I know he'll take me to my dad. My dad who says miracles happen in hospitals every day. I'm sure Innocent will be one more.

One more miracle.

Mr. Malola holds open a door. The old man and the baby disappear through it. "Your father knocked off several hours ago, Clare," he says. "The cell phone is good for light but not for calls, so I cannot contact your daddy for you."

What is this man talking about? My father said he was working today. I'll have to run back into the operating room and find him myself. I don't have time for this nonsense. Innocent doesn't have time. But I can't get through the doorway because Mr. Malola grabs my arm. "Your daddy has gone home," he says.

I stare at the empty space between his two front teeth. "Home?"

Mr. Malola nods.

But now we're at the hospital. That's what's important. We're at the hospital. Someone will help us. Someone has to.

"Malaria!" I scream. My head burns. I'm furious. "See that boy? He has malaria. Or pneumonia. Something bad!"

"I'm afraid he must wait," Mr. Malola says, and sighs. "We are overcrowded. I shall bring acetaminophen."

I might not be a doctor, but I sure know what that big word means.

"What?" I say. "You're going to bring pills for a regular old fever?"

Mr. Malola has already gone, so again, I move past the people. Past a baby with skin stretched like Saran Wrap over his ribs. Past a girl who looks like a skeleton. Past a man asleep on the floor. To Memory, who looks up at me, her eyes searching, wide.

"The clinical officer will bring a pill," I say. I don't tell her it's a pill that won't fight malaria. I don't tell her that after everything, my father isn't even here. But Saidi knows something is dreadfully wrong. He takes my wrist and pulls me outside, where I heave out a huge sob and share the news.

"Where is your daddy?" Saidi asks.

"Home," I say. "Waiting for me."

Saidi leads me across the lot to the mopeds. I'm too shaky to drive, so I get on the back of his bike and hold on to him tight.

We're at my house in no time. I pound the front door. There's no answer. I grab my key out of my back pocket, but my hands are trembling so badly that it takes three tries before I can fit the key in the lock and open it.

When I do, it's too quiet. Too dark. "Dad!" I shout as we dash inside. My voice bounces off the walls. I check my watch: 8:15. I flip on the light switch, bolt to Dad's bedroom, and yell for him over and over, even though it's totally obvious: he's not here.

161

"Clare!" Saidi calls.
I run to the kitchen, where he holds up a note:

Clare—
Where are you?
Stay put. Gone to look.
Dad

Sweat drips down my forehead.
Cold sweat.
I'm chilled to the bone.

CHAPTER 28

Even though Saidi cuts the motor at the road, the people who live near the edge of Mkumba village hear the moped and run out of their huts, startled by the noise.

Saidi talks to a few teenagers, who point to a group of men sitting by a fire playing a game of bawo. We race over to them. Sparks spit at our knees while Saidi asks if they've seen the doctor.

One of the men looks up. "Kapoloma," he says.

The smoke burns my nose.

"Next village," Saidi tells me, and we sprint back to the bike.

We get to Kapoloma village in a few minutes. We ditch the moped on a patch of dirt and bolt toward the huts. Before we reach them, though, three women walk by. One carries a pot in her hand.

"*Adokotala ali kuti?*" Saidi asks.

The women talk to each other like they're washing dishes by the river, like we've got all day.

"Let's go!" I whisper.

The lady with the pot taps a crooked finger against her forehead and points to the other side of the village. Across the field, a bunch of little boys are drumming under the stars. When we get closer, Saidi shouts out to ask if anyone has seen the doctor. The boys stop their music. "*Chauko,*" one says, and points to a nearby hut.

In seconds, we're panting outside of it. Other than the pit latrines, it's the first hut I've seen with an actual door. Saidi bangs on it.

But the village chief doesn't open the door. My father does. He looks frantic. He grabs my shoulders, shakes me hard. "Where were you?" he yells. "I was worried sick."

There's a slow *clunk, clunk, clunk* as the chief lumbers over.

And I'm still trying to remember how Mom's skin felt the last day I ever saw her. She was in the hospital bed. I reached over and held her hand. *But was it warm or cold? Warm or cold?* I'm desperate to remember, but I can't.

We tell Dad about Innocent.

"Meet us at the hospital," Dad says to Saidi.

Then Dad and I bolt to the Land Rover, which is parked in a ditch across the road. Dirt whirs under the car wheels and the night wraps me up. We turn off the main road onto the narrow path.

I see a dot of light.

A dot of life.

The hospital.

I close my eyes
I hear Dad.
"IV drip!"
"Wrap blankets."
"Twenty milligrams."
I hear Dad.
"Save this boy!"
I hear Dad.
"I saved him!"
I hear Dad
in my mind.

As soon as we burst into the hospital, I point to Innocent, who's still curled up on Memory's lap in the corner. Dad walks over, puts his hand on Memory's back. She nods, and Dad lifts Innocent and carries him across the waiting room.

Memory and I follow them down the unlit hallway into the pediatric ward. Except for the IV drips, it hardly feels like a hospital. It reeks of chlorine. The beds—slabs of wood with thin mats—are full of tiny children, two or three on each one. A red number is spray-painted on the white wall above each bed.

Dad sets Innocent down on bed number eight, right beside a little girl. He disappears into the hallway and returns with a pair of rubber gloves and a stethoscope. After he listens to Innocent's heart, he pulls up Innocent's eyelids one at a time.

I shudder. For a second, Innocent looks dead.

Dad calls to the nurse, who's on the other side of the

ward placing a blue mask over the face of a baby. A tube connects the baby's mask to a bag the nurse has in her hand. She opens and shuts her fist. Opens and shuts it, trying to send air from the bag into the baby's lungs.

With the other hand, the nurse holds up a finger, telling us to wait. But we can't wait. Not a blink, not a heartbeat, not a breath. Doesn't she know?

Dad pricks Innocent's finger, draws blood.

Then, *clang!* The nurse wheels a metal pole across the room. The pole has a bag filled with liquid attached to the top of it. Memory and I scramble to the end of bed number eight, out of the nurse's way. We watch her push a long needle into Innocent's arm and tape it there so it won't fall out.

"He's getting fluids now," Dad tells us. "The blood test will be done soon. Then we'll know what type."

"What type?" I say, not understanding.

I look at Memory. Her eyes are wide. She is very still.

"What type of malaria. I'm afraid Innocent has malaria. He's in a coma."

"That's it?" I scream. "That's all you can do? Give him some fluids?" Here's Innocent in a hospital bed, lips parched, eyes half shut. The boy who cried because he thought I was a ghost. The boy with the dimples who stared at my freckles. The boy who stood in the standard one doorway, arms and legs stretched wide, blocking my escape. I wanted to run from Innocent that day. But I'll never run from him now. "Do something!" I shout. I'm burning up. Really burning up. "Operate! Give him a shot!"

Dad puts his arms around Memory and me as the nurse slips a blue mask onto Innocent's face.

166

CHAPTER 29

The chills are back. The nurse says to ride them. I ride them.

Around and around.

I close my eyes, watch them prick circles around my belly. Around my back. All around me. I'm freezing. Freezing cold. "The window," I say. I think I said it. "The window." But my lips are stuck together. Dry.

When I wake again, I'm burning. I remember the lake. A lake of boiling water. A big lake of hot Banja tea. I'm falling. Into the lake.

Falling.

"Save me," I say. I think I said it.

"Sweetie," Mom says. She has a paintbrush in her hand. She sets it down next to the canvas on the easel. There's a basket of apples on a table. Mom's painting a still life. Back to basics, after so long.

I inhale acrylics. I love that smell. The smell of desert turquoise, lemon yellow, Mars black. The smell of secret colors no one knows but us.

Mom kisses the top of my head. She sets a cool washcloth on my forehead. "Quite a day!" she says, and laughs, a deep belly laugh.

Mom's always here when it counts.

Count sheep.

Count scorpions.

Count all the wild beasts while my ears ring, ring, ring.

Later, I wake up in a puddle of sweat. A breeze blows through the window. Dad sits in a chair beside me. "It's horrible," he says into his cell phone. "The worst."

I swallow. Well, I try to swallow. But I can't. I reach for my phone. I need to call Memory. To tell her the news: I'm dead.

Maybe it will be too much.

I cry a tear. At least, I think I do. I stick my tongue out to taste it, but it isn't there.

"Hey, Mom," I say.

She turns from the canvas.

"If a tear falls and no one feels it, did it fall?"

Mom smiles. "Great artists ask great questions," she says, and turns back to her painting.

No more apples.

Only planets.

And stars.

CHAPTER 30

It takes a few days, but eventually I realize that it wasn't me who died.

"Where am I?" I ask.

"Sun Private Hospital, Clare, in Blantyre." Dad takes my hand. "I'm so sorry, but Innocent died that night. There's nothing else we could have done. You passed out, so I brought you here."

My heart cracks along the same lines where it was just starting to heal from my mother's death. Tears pour down my face. I'm a river. A river of tears. There's nothing holding my sorrow inside anymore. No skin. No bones. There are no borders to my pain. It's everywhere. It's in me. Around me. On the metal rails of the hospital bed. In the cardboard hospital toast. I inhale it five times a day through the oxygen concentrator until Dad and I finally talk—really talk—about what happened.

The tests show that I have pneumonia. "You were probably sick before you even went to the lake. That cough you had wasn't allergies. It was something called walking pneumonia. Looks like you were carrying the virus around in your lungs." Dad says that soaring down the road on the moped swallowing dust turned the virus into something more serious. "I feel awful," he says. "I should've known."

At night the nurse comes to give me pills. I swallow them and drink the tiny cup of water, but I'm still thirsty and the nurse has already gone. Dad's next to me, dozing in the chair beside the bed. "Dad!" I say. "Dad!" He doesn't move, so I reach out and touch his elbow. He still doesn't stir, so I poke him a few times in the arm.

"Mmmm."

"Water, Dad. I need water."

"Right, right." He jumps up. "Water." He dashes into the hall.

Sun Private Hospital is night-and-day different from the government-run hospital where Dad works in Machinga. Here, patients get their own rooms, plenty of medicine, and food from the cafeteria. So why didn't Dad bring Innocent to this private hospital along with me? Is it only because I'm a doctor's daughter that I can get this kind of special treatment? Or is it because I'm a *mzungu*? If I had stayed in the Machinga District Hospital, would I be dead too?

Dad returns from the hallway with a whole bottle of water. I take a few sips. "*Zikomo*, Dad," I say. I feel hot all over. I've been in the hospital four days already. Four days too long. I need to get out, so I ask him: "Why'd you leave Innocent at the hospital in Machinga?"

"What, honey?" Dad sits down.

I cough. "Why'd you leave Innocent there?"

He reaches over and holds my hand.

"Why didn't you bring him to this hospital? With us?" Thinking about Innocent, I feel too heavy to move.

"Clare," Dad says, "it's complicated. And besides, even though we got him breathing again, he'd slipped into a coma. It was too dangerous to transport him then."

Innocent's voice plays in my ears—*I one the cake . . . I eight the cake*—and his laugh, like wind chimes, when he finally figures out what that means.

CHAPTER 31

I've already missed Innocent's funeral, which is bad enough. Now I'm desperate to get back to the village to check on Memory, but Dad says that's out of the question. "You've got to take it easy, honey. A few more days on the oxygen. You know your lungs haven't cleared all the way."

"A few more days!" I feel like a dead leaf being stepped on again and again. Mr. Special Kingsley will have to tell the standard one students that our play is canceled. We've missed so many days of rehearsal. Besides, I would never recast Innocent's role. I can't even imagine what that would do to Memory. To me.

"Pneumonia's serious stuff," Dad says.

Every morning after I get hooked up to the oxygen machine, Dad and I spend hours playing checkers and Othello, the two games the hospital keeps on hand. In the afternoons, he drives to the Royal Malawi Hotel to rest for a few hours while I sketch in the pad he brought me. But each time I try to force myself to draw, my pen drifts off the page along with my mind.

Today Dad returns from the hotel with a big smile on his face. "I've got something here that's going to cheer you up," he says. He opens his briefcase and takes out a stack of paper. "A messenger delivered these to the hotel. They're for you."

He fixes the pillows behind my head so I can get a better look. My Bingo cards! They've been turned into get-well cards for me. Each and every one has a message on the back.

On the top of the pile is a card that says:

You are missed by your classmates and students. Take good care. Your headmaster, Mr. Special Kingsley

I can't believe so many people at Mzanga have noticed I'm gone. I want to flip through them all to see if Saidi has written me a note, but my father is watching, so I turn over the cards in order from top to bottom. Every once in a while, I read one out loud.

Sickness wrote:

Please fele betta. Love from your friend, Sickness

On the other side of the paper, she drew a scarf around the head of the lion I sketched on the Bingo board.

Norman's card says:

Coud you find a flute in Blantyre for me wen u feel better?

Halfway through the stack, I see a card from Saidi. It says:

Best wishes to feel well in quickest time. Your friend Saidi

I read it over twice before I look at the next one. I'm almost at the bottom of the pile when my throat tightens. I haven't seen a card from Memory yet. I turn over the very last one. It's from a girl named Jelly. I don't even know who she is. All it says is:

I like dog. Jelly, std. 4

I cry. I can't help it. I'm afraid Memory hates me. If I were her, I'd hate me too. Hate me because of where I was born, how much money I have, and how I get treated to a whole other kind of medicine, a whole other chance at life. But when I tell Dad why I'm crying, he says, "Think of what she's going through, Clare."

And suddenly I burn with shame at how selfish I am to even think she could make a card for me, when she's probably having enough trouble just waking up in the morning. I know that after Mom died, whenever I opened my eyes, I would get confused and think, *This has got to be the nightmare. Now let me wake up to my real life.*

After seven days in the hospital, when I finally do get back home, I run to the veranda and find Fred burrowed in the corner of the puffy green chair. As soon as Fred sees me, she flaps her wings. I plop down and she flies onto my lap. "I missed you so much," I whisper, and nuzzle my cheek into her silky feathers. I never thought a chicken could hold her own in a conversation, but Fred starts squawking up a storm. When she finishes catching me up on her life, she prances across the floor and settles in the corner, where I know she's laying an egg for me.

"I'll be back to check on you," I say. Then I go into my bedroom. The scarves draping my dresser look so happy and colorful, like a little rainbow right in my room. I lift the netting and climb onto the mattress. It's still thin, but it's my bed and it feels good, so I lie there and stare at the mosquito netting around me. Then I think and think and think about what happened and what I can say to Memory, since no hug, no kind words, nothing at all can vaccinate her from the pain of losing her brother. But maybe if I tell her about my mom, she won't feel so alone. I wonder if her mother liked to laugh like mine, or if her father told bad jokes.

I'm in the middle of praying that Memory will speak to me again when I hear Mrs. Bwanali's booming voice. "My girl come home!" I heave myself out of bed. We meet up in the living room and she swallows me in a huge hug. "My girl, my girl," she says, and wipes a tear from the corner of her eye. "You look healthy like a water buffalo!" She throws her head back and laughs and laughs and laughs. She takes my hand and pulls me into the kitchen, where a chocolate cake is sitting on the table. "Dr. Heath special recipe," she says. "I make to fatten your belly after illness. To turn you strong."

If cake can make me strong, I'm all for it! "*Zikomo kwambiri,*" I croak. Then I throw my arms around Mrs.

Bwanali and hug her as tightly as I can, which isn't much, since my arms are about as muscley as two strands of thread.

Mrs. Bwanali sits down for cake and tea with Dad and me. "Very yummy!" she says after the first bite.

"Who taught you that word?" I ask, teasing.

"My girl, Clare, of course," she says, and smiles. "Now tell me the scary story. What happen to you?"

So I tell her all about how I woke up in the hospital and heard the sad news about Innocent, how my heart broke, and how I couldn't even concentrate enough to draw. I tell her how I used the oxygen concentrator five times every day, and how Dad stayed at my side almost the whole time. While I'm telling my scary story, Mrs. Bwanali helps herself to another piece of her cake. And when she helps herself to a third, it's all Dad and I can do not to burst into giggles.

"So, what about you?" I ask. "What's been happening here?"

Mrs. Bwanali puts her hands behind her head. Then she gives me a behavior report on Fred, who was not excellent or even satisfactory. "I try to care for this *nkhuku* Fred while you are away and ill," she says. "But this chicken look at me like this." Mrs. Bwanali cocks her head to the side and scowls. "I tell Fred, 'Clare is in hospital. We must pray together.' And we do. We shut eyes and pray. This chicken only give one egg in whole week."

While Mrs. Bwanali complains about Fred, I finally get a chance to eat her cake. It really is delicious!

"This chicken scratch up the furniture and go to the ladies' right on the veranda floor even after I put her in

176

the box." Mrs. Bwanali shakes her head like she still can't believe how bad Fred was. "This chicken Fred was so mad and sad without her friend Clare. This chicken need her own pit latrine! It is good you come home, Clare, because me and this chicken—we cannot survive long in same house without you."

After cake and tea, Mrs. Bwanali leaves for the market and Dad drives me to Mkumba village, where I give Memory's grandmother a hug and tell her how terribly sorry I am. Then I walk in the plum-colored dusk down to the river, where Memory is washing the dinner dishes.

When Memory sees me, she picks up a dirty pot and hands it over. I squat beside her on the riverbank, take a rag from a bucket, and scrub, scrub, scrub, harder and harder, until I work up the guts.

"Do you hate me?" I finally ask.

"Hate you?" Memory stops scrubbing.

"Well . . . hate my dad?"

She looks at me hard. "It is not fair," she says. "This world is not fair." She bites her lip and knits her eyebrows together.

My heart drums in my ears. I want to tell her that it's not my fault. That I didn't mean for it to be this way. That I wanted to save Innocent, and my father did too. It's just that he couldn't. Dad couldn't. Things weren't set up that way.

But Memory is the number one student for a reason. She already understands. She already knows there's a system in place, and we can't change it overnight. We can only do our small part, and take one step at a time, even if that step involves tangling with the law. "I love that you steal electric bicycle to try to save my brother," Memory says. She puts the pot on the muddy bank and wraps me in a hug.

Memory pulls away from me. "There is a secret," she says.

"Secret?" I wipe my cheek.

She leans in close and whispers, "Electric bicycles got stolen from the hospital parking lot."

I gasp.

She puts a finger over her lips and says, "Shhh!" She hugs me again. "*Ndimakukonda*," she says. "I love you."

"*Ndimakukonda*," I say, because, of course, I love her too. And even though we've only known each other about a month, I could swear we've been friends our whole lives.

CHAPTER 32

I can't wait another second to get back to school. I haven't had a fever for three days, so when Dad shakes me awake Monday morning, I get right out of bed. The buttery smell of pancakes fills the whole house, and as I pull my uniform over my head, I can already hear Mrs. Bwanali explode, "Clare, love. You look pretty as a wild-cat!" The uniform is bigger than ever on me, so today I have to wrap the scarf twice around my waist in order to gather all the extra fabric.

I shuffle down the hall and through the living room and stand in the kitchen doorway, feeling a little groggy and a bit weak but otherwise not too bad.

Mrs. Bwanali takes one look at me. "My girl. My pretty, pretty girl," she says. She runs across the tiny kitchen, throws her arms around me, and wraps me in a warm hug.

While Dad chows down his pancakes, Mrs. Bwanali

checks me out one more time. She leans forward and examines my eyebrows, my ears, my nose. She clucks her teeth. "Open the mouth," she orders. "Put the tongue outside."

But when I do what she says, Mrs. Bwanali's face sags. She shakes her head. "Dr. Silver," she says, "yoo-hoo, Dr. Silver!" She waves her hand in front of Dad's medical report.

Dad looks up. "What is it?"

"My pretty girl, Miss Clare, not much pretty this morning. This throat is red as the backside of baboon."

"I'm fine," I say.

"Bad spirits fight inside this body," Mrs. Bwanali tells Dad before she turns to me and says, "In the bed, my girl."

"What? I'm going to—"

She puts her hand on her hip. "Mrs. Bwanali know when a girl can go to the school, when she can go to a party, when she can go to the trading center," she says. "Clare, you must go in the bed."

"Dad!" I say.

"She hasn't had a fever for three days," Dad says, like he's mildly interested in helping me out.

"Show your daddy. Stick this tongue out like a lizard, Clare."

I do, and the two of them stare down my throat.

"Red bumps," Mrs. Bwanali tells Dad. "Bad spirit."

Dad nods. "There is still some slight inflammation," he says. "That's to be expected."

"When you are at work, Dr. Silver, I am chief of this village, no?"

A bead of sweat dribbles down the side of my face.

"I think one more day of rest would be good," Dad tells me. "It's certainly not going to hurt you any."

"If I don't get back to school, my students will never learn the English alphabet before we leave this country," I say.

"There is more than one way to cook a goat," Mrs. Bwanali says.

I shiver.

"Or a chicken!" Dad says, and laughs.

"Not funny," I tell him. Dad's still not a big fan of Fred's, especially since Mrs. Bwanali gave the report about how badly Fred behaved while I was in the hospital.

"I have to go to school today. I have to see my friends!" I say.

"A true friend shall wait for the other through the hungry season," Mrs. Bwanali tells me. "Now go!" she says, gently pushing me through the doorway as Dad calls out, "Bye, kid."

Back in my bedroom, I'm steaming mad. I stick the thermometer in my mouth only to find that Mrs. Bwanali's right: my fever's back up to ninety-nine and a half. Plus, whenever I swallow, it feels like someone's scraping my throat with sandpaper. I take off my uniform and spend the morning drinking tea, sketching all the foods I miss, and flipping through the pages of *Gallery Geek*, a magazine of super-hip modern art that I brought all the way here. After an hour or two of hanging out in my bed and chewing on my necklace, I close my eyes and fall asleep.

Mom visits. She sits on the edge of my bed stroking my hair, admiring my uniform, which is hanging from the nail on the wall. "That pendant I made you. I'm glad you put a dent in it," she says. "Why should it be perfect? Perfect is boring."

I wonder if Mom knows we stole the mopeds. That wasn't exactly a boring thing to do. I'm pretty certain she's clueless about the fact that I'm now a teenage criminal. If she did know, I doubt she'd look so peaceful, so calm.

When I wake up from my nap, I'm ravished. I trudge back to the kitchen, where Mrs. Bwanali's dicing a tomato at the counter. "How you feel now, Clare?" she asks. No sooner have the words left her mouth than her eyes bulge. She slowly walks toward me, feels my cheek, and then yanks her hand away like she's touched a hot stove.

"What?" I shout.

"Mark from the . . . from the . . ."

"Mark from the what?" I shriek.

Her eyes fill with tears. "Evil spirit!" she whispers.

I fly to the bathroom and check in the mirror. There, printed on my cheek, is an upside-down, melting strawberry ice cream cone. It sort of looks like a machete dripping blood. I run my finger over it. Then I laugh out loud. I laugh so hard that I can't even stand up anymore. I run to my room, push aside the netting, and flop down onto my bed.

Mrs. Bwanali pokes her head in the door. "I know the witch who do this to you. He come in the door when I scrub clothes outside. I must shut door to keep out this witch! My poor, poor Clare."

Before the woman collapses from guilt, I show her the picture I drew in my sketchbook. I try to explain that I must have fallen asleep right on top of the page with the ice cream cone, but Mrs. Bwanali's still convinced I've been cursed. So I pull her into the bathroom, pour some water onto a washcloth, and scrub the ink off my cheek. "See," I say. "It's not the mark of a wicked witch. It's from my red pen."

"Oh!" Mrs. Bwanali says. She throws her hands over her mouth and then rubs her thumb across my clean cheek to make sure the mark of the sorcerer is really gone. When she sees that it is, she laughs her thunderous laugh and her whole body jiggles.

CHAPTER 33

Memory told me that Saidi told her we'd better figure out a way to replace the mopeds that got stolen. She said Saidi is trying to come up with a plan, but so far, no luck. The more I think about the fact that we're practically criminals, the itchier my muscles feel and the more I've got to stretch my legs. For two days, I've been in bed doing nothing but sketching, thinking, dreaming, and swallowing medicine for my sore throat, and suddenly, I can't take it anymore.

I get out of bed, untie one of the five scarves that are still draped over my dresser, and twist it into a ring. I fasten the ends of the ring with two barrettes and set the ring on my head. I carefully balance one issue of *Gallery Geek* on top of the ring. As I cross my bedroom, I remember how Marcella and I used to practice walking like fashion models whenever we had downtime during play rehearsals.

"Walk and swivel, walk and swivel," she would coach as I strutted down the long hallway behind the stage.

Now all that practice with Marcella is coming in handy, because I make it halfway across my bedroom before the magazine slides off my head to the floor.

By Wednesday morning, when Mrs. Bwanali crashes through the door, I've made a lot of progress. I'm walking across the house in my pink pajamas balancing Dad's medical book plus four magazines on my head. Mrs. Bwanali takes one look at me, crosses herself, and says, "Stick the tongue outside."

I do, and both she and Dad stare down my throat while I wait for the verdict. I haven't had a fever since Monday, so I'm hoping for good news.

"Looks clear to me," Dad says. "What do you think?"

Mrs. Bwanali smiles. "I think this girl getting dumb, dumb, dumb. She cannot stay here with me today. She be in my way. Do you understand? I must wash floors. I must clean curtains. Dr. Silver, drive this healthy girl to school. Today!"

"Yes, ma'am," Dad says.

"Hallelujah!" I shout. I bolt to the bathroom, jump in the shower, and comb the last bit of *après-shampooing lissant* through my hair. I can't wait to see my students. I can't wait to see my friends! I throw on my beautiful uniform, hug Mrs. Bwanali, and run outside.

A few minutes later, Dad parks at the top of the hill and gets out of the Land Rover. "Where are you going?" I ask. As I step out, my legs feel a little wobbly.

"I want to have a word with Mr. Kingsley," Dad says. "Let him know if you're not feeling good, he should send a messenger to the hospital and I'll come around to pick you up. Do you have your lunch?"

"Got it," I say. I've packed a grilled cheese sandwich Dad made for me himself and also a bottle of water. Dad said that even though the other students don't eat lunch at school, I have to—doctor's orders! He says he'll tell Mr. Special Kingsley. Around noon I'm supposed to ask Mrs. Tomasi to use the ladies'. That way the other kids won't be jealous that I'm leaving class to eat. Once I get outside, I can hide behind the trunk of the blue gum tree and have my sandwich.

"The water?" Dad asks.

"Got it," I say.

Dad rubs the top of my sweaty head. Then we both walk down the hill. When we cross the schoolyard, I glance at the standard one classroom block. I miss my students so much. Today I'm going to teach them the ABC song. I just hope Mr. Special Kingsley has broken the news: After missing seven days of rehearsal, and with Innocent gone, our production is over before it even began.

Memory, Patuma, Winnie, Stella, and Sickness are all standing by the flagpole, so I say a quick goodbye to Dad and run to my friends. We hug tight for a long time. "We miss you a lot," Sickness says.

Saidi comes over, the soccer ball in his hands. "You survived! You look good." My friends giggle.

Saidi rolls his eyes. "I mean, she look healthy," he says, and gallops back to the soccer game. I watch him dribble the ball down the field.

"You love Saidi?" Patuma asks.

"No. No!" I say. I can't love Saidi, because Memory does.

"Do you like Norman?" I reply.

Patuma smiles shyly and looks at the ground.

"I must warn you, my poor friend," Sickness says. "Agnes is more angry than ever in her life."

"Angry at me?" I shiver.

"She say you leave her at the lake with no money to transport home."

I gasp. Agnes's bus fare home was the last thing on my mind that day.

"She must bake twelve *chikondamoyo* cakes for the minibus driver to pay for free ride back," Stella explains.

"Is she mad at Memory too?" I ask.

"No, Agnes forgive Memory," Winnie says. "She feel sorry for the death."

That's when we all look over at Memory. She isn't even listening to our chatter. She's staring across the schoolyard at nobody. At nothing.

All of us girls exchange a look. Then I throw my arm around Memory on one side, and Sickness holds her hand on the other. "*Tiyeni*," I say, and together, the bunch of us get going to class.

When Mrs. Tomasi spots us coming through the doorway, she claps her hands together and smiles. "Clare!" she says. "What a glorious blessing! The Lord has delivered you."

I slide onto the bench next to Agnes. "Hi, Agnes," I say, figuring it's as good a time as any to start fresh. But Agnes won't even look at me.

Mrs. Tomasi assigns everyone chores before handing me a list of new vocabulary words. But I'm not the same girl I was the last time I was here at Mzanga Full Primary School. I leave the paper on the table and grab a grass broom from the pile in the corner. I've just begun to sweep the floor along with Memory and Stella when Mrs. Tomasi tries to snatch the broom right out of my hands. "You must rest," she says, tugging at the broomstick. My cheeks feel flushed.

"I want to," I say, and tug back. "I want to clean." And for some strange reason, I really do. But I know she's right. It's too soon, and I don't want to land myself back in the hospital again, so I let go.

At the daily assembly, I line up on the field between Memory and Sickness. When the standard one students frolic onto the grass, I get a huge lump in my throat. I miss Innocent so much that it takes a few seconds before I notice a man standing at the front of the standard one line. He's wearing a blue sport coat and tie. It looks like the District Education Office finally sent a new teacher. I guess I won't be teaching the ABC song after all.

I heave out only one sob before a hand takes mine. I turn. It's Memory. She looks away, but not before I spot a tear weaving its way down her cheek, and I hear a tiny voice shout, "*Mzungu!* Clare!" The standard one students break out of line and run to me. In twos and threes they welcome me back with warm hugs and Chichewan whispers.

Mr. Special Kingsley limps over. "Welcome back to Mzanga, Clare," he says. "I did intend to explain to you that a new teacher has arrived for our standard one students, but there was a problem with bullfrogs." He gives an embarrassed grin and stares at the ground. "Bullfrogs create . . . bullfrog babies underneath my office floor," he says. "And therefore, I try to move bullfrogs and was delayed in reaching you with this message."

I sniffle and little Felicity wraps her arms around my waist.

"You are loved, Clare," Mr. Special Kingsley says, and smiles. "We are all drinking from the fountain of joy that you have returned to us. We do hope that you and Memory shall resume the practice of the show with the children now."

"Oh, sir," I say. I pat Felicity on the head and she runs across the field to line up with her standard one classmates. "There's no way we can do the play now," I say. "I mean, we couldn't. We've missed so much practice. How would we ever teach the kids their lines, make the costumes, and build a set? There's hardly any time left."

I'm completely freaking out, when Memory taps my shoulder and glares at me, her eyes hard like pebbles. "The children have lost a classmate," she says. "They shall not also lose their show."

"Of course we shall do the play, Clare," Mr. Special Kingsley continues. "The chiefs have already issued invitations. The villagers are buzzing with excitement. We cannot cancel. I have made arrangements with the new standard one teacher so that you two girls shall resume the practice schedule as it was before."

Memory stares at her flip-flops. "I . . . I cannot work on the play," she says. "Only Clare now."

My heart is in my throat. It will be hard enough for me

to step back into that classroom and work on the show Innocent helped us write. I can't even imagine what it would be like for Memory. No one argues with her. It will be me in charge. Me all alone.

After assembly, Memory and I trudge back to the standard eight classroom in silence and misery. We've both untied the scarves around our waists, since we won't be needing to look like teachers anymore.

No sooner do we pass over the threshold than we catch wind of a fight.

"When was your uniform purchased?" Agnes shouts at Saidi's back. "Standard two?"

It's true. Saidi's pants stop at his shins, and his shirt is so tight it looks like the buttons will pop off any minute.

"Your uniform is so old that it shall fit an ant," Agnes says. "No one wants to marry a poor farm boy such as you, Saidi!"

"Be quiet, Agnes," Memory says, but Agnes won't stop.

"I shall marry a businessman in the city," Agnes announces while my useless tongue rolls over in my mouth like an echo with nothing to say. I may be speechless, but that won't stop me from making my feelings known. I slip onto the bench and lift my hand like I have to scratch an itch on my forehead. Then I jab Agnes in the ribs with my elbow while Saidi cranes his neck over a book Norman has open on the table.

"Visit the seamstress," Agnes shouts at Saidi's back. "Mrs. Kumwenda shall make you look better."

Suddenly, there's a strange sound at the back of the room.

Mrs. Tomasi stands in the doorway clearing her throat, wrapped in a bright orange and red dress, looking just like a fire-breathing dragon. And I guess it doesn't matter what country you live in, teachers will go to desperate measures to get your attention, whether it's by slamming a yardstick against the chalkboard like Mr. Papasanassi did back in fourth grade or by sneaking up on you and scaring you to death with silence.

Mrs. Tomasi glares at us for a full minute, and when she finally speaks, her voice is calm and low. "Old Helix was the eldest spider in all the bush," she says. I pinch the extra fabric of my uniform at the waist and think about how I'd like to clock Agnes.

"The old spider was older than the *malambe* tree," Mrs. Tomasi says. "The old spider was even older than the purple sky. One day, Old Helix got so old that his legs ached when he crawled across the savannah. This made him grumpier than even the crocodile."

A warm wind blows through the doorway. I reach up and run my hand over my hair. It feels like straw. It's definitely going to rain.

"In the morning, the wife of Old Helix woke her husband. '*Muli bwanji?*' she asked, inquiring how he was."

After a couple minutes, I forget about Agnes and I forget about my hair. All I can picture is Old Helix.

"'You are a bad wife. A mean wife,' Old Helix replied to the spider who had cooked his food, sewn his clothes, and raised his five thousand children for six hundred years."

Our eyes follow Mrs. Tomasi as she slowly walks to the front of the classroom. "At the beginning, the wife was gentle with her husband. For she understood that he had reason to be grumpy. 'Please be kind,' she said. 'Remember, I have cooked your food, sewn your clothes, and raised your five thousand children for six hundred years.'

"Old Helix only grunted. Morning after morning, when the wife of Old Helix would ask, '*Muli bwanji?*' the husband would taunt her. 'You are an ugly wife. A dirty wife. A bad wife.'

"One day, the spider wife could bear it no longer. At night, under a swollen moon, she crawled across the bush to find her mother, who was thousands of years older than she herself. The spider wife shook her mother awake. 'My husband aches. His body is sore. Yet he is a mean spider. What shall I do?'

"The mother itched her front legs together. Then she advised her daughter. The next morning, when Old Helix awoke, he knew something was wrong—something more than the pain in his joints or the pull in his jowl. When he tried to button his shirt, he realized what it was. 'Where is my leg?' he wailed with shock.

"The wife of Old Helix held the leg of her husband in her mouth. She dropped it at his feet. 'Here is your leg, my good, kind, faithful husband. You have seven more.'

"The spider wife looked at her husband with gentle eyes, for she did not mean to hurt him, but she was wise and had followed the advice of her mother. 'Remember, husband,' she said, 'if you want to keep what is yours, you must protect what is ours.' And with that, the wife of Old

Helix left her aching husband a lighter burden to carry across the bush floor."

A faint smile crosses Mrs. Tomasi's lips. "Agnes, rise," she says.

Memory leans over and sticks her shoulder into mine. The two of us exchange gleeful stares, like two witches about to watch a frog boil in a scalding-hot cauldron.

"So, what shall we learn from this?" Mrs. Tomasi asks.

Agnes studies the tabletop. "I learned we shall respect each other," she mumbles.

"Very good," Mrs. Tomasi says.

A few minutes later, we go outside for science. We're going to learn about birds. Saidi is standing with his arms crossed, staring out at the soccer field.

I go over to him. "Don't worry," I say. "I'll sew you a new uniform."

"I hate school," he says. Then he kicks a rock so hard that he cuts open his big toe and it bleeds all over the dirt.

CHAPTER 34

The bullfrogs are croaking up a storm, Fred is pecking at the sunflower seeds, and Dad and I are sipping limeade on the veranda. "Did any of your patients ever admit to giving you Fred?" I ask.

"Nope," Dad says. "Still a mystery." He takes a piece of paper out of his pocket. "On a more urgent matter," he says, unfolding the sheet. "This letter was delivered to the hospital."

He hands it over:

To the American Doctor:

Your daughter told me you work at Machinga District Hospital. I don't know her name, but it is a fact that while visiting Lake Malombe, she and her friends stole two mopeds from my property. Though

you are not your brother's keeper, you are your
daughter's. Either replace the mopeds (deliverable to the
Chomp and Chew Stop) or I'll be forced to press
charges with the authorities.

> *Yours sincerely,*
> *Derek Witmore*
> *Owner, The Chomp and Chew Stop*
> *Lake Malombe*

"Press charges?" I scoop Fred off the floor. "Will I be
in . . ." I can hardly stand to say the words. "Solitary con-
finement?" The letter shakes in my hand. Everyone knows
that prison food is even worse than hospital food. Plus, the
uniforms in jail are bound to be uglier than the uniforms
at school.

"Don't worry, Clare. Tell me where Saidi put the
mopeds. I'll drive them back to this Derek fellow," Dad
says.

I suck up the rest of the limeade with the straw—every
last drop—before I break the news. "They were stolen," I
admit. "The night we brought Innocent to you, someone
swiped them from the hospital parking lot."

Dad rubs the stubble on his chin. "That does present a
bit of a dilemma. I guess in that case I'll have to buy two
brand-new mopeds."

"You don't have to bail me out, Dad."

"It's a small price to pay. I'm just thankful you're okay.
Really, it's no problem, kid."

Maybe it's not a problem for him, but it is for me. I
spend hours trying to think of a plan so that Memory,

Saidi, and I can buy back the mopeds ourselves, and every two minutes I make another suggestion.

"I know! We could sell groundnuts in the trading center."

"Wouldn't make enough profit," Dad says, swirling his straw in his drink.

"We could work in the hospital."

"Child labor laws, plus too much disease."

But then Dad suggests that maybe the three of us can volunteer for the hospital without actually going inside it, and he could compensate us for our work. "You know, cooking food for the orphans. Something along those lines."

In the morning while I'm brushing my teeth, I come up with an even better idea. Dad says he's going to send a messenger with a note to let Derek know our plan.

Dad insists on driving me to school, even though I really am feeling completely fine. When I get there, I walk down the hill and find Memory hanging out in the school-yard with Patuma and Winnie. First, I spill the bad news about Derek's letter. I think we were all praying that he'd forget to track us down, even though in the back of our minds, we knew that sooner or later this day would come. Before Memory's jaw hits the field grass, I give her some desperately needed encouragement. "Not to worry!" I say. "We can be our own saviors. I have a plan."

But when I tell her we're going to paint murals to decorate the hospital wards and cheer up the patients, Memory looks like an evil spirit really has landed on me.

"Never mind," I say. "It was a stupid idea." How could I ask her to return to the very same place where her brother died? My face burns with humiliation. "I'm so stupid! I'll think of something else. I promise I will. There's got to be something else we can do to buy—"

Memory throws back her shoulders. "I shall do it," she says.

"What?" I say. "No." I grab her hand. "I won't let you."

"For Innocent," she says. "That is what he want, I know. To make other children smile like he do always."

"Really?" I say.

Memory nods once.

"If you change your mind . . ."

"Change the mind?" Winnie says. She whispers something to Patuma in Chichewa, and the two of them giggle. "We change from our school dresses to the *chitenje* when we gather the firewood. We change the bathwater. But change the mind? Perhaps the sorcerer might perform such a trick, but Memory, she is not the sorcerer," Winnie says, and giggles again.

"Anyone can change their mind," I say. "You decide to do something different. That's all it means."

"I decide I shall do this," Memory says. "I shall do this job. I have the power to change the mind. However, I choose to keep the mind. Now, where is that boy, Saidi?" she says, scouring the soccer field. "We must share the plan with him as well."

"Saidi shall not return to school," Winnie says.

"What?" I say.

Memory gasps.

"Just because of what Agnes said about his uniform?" I ask.

Patuma nods.

"Many children leave school due to improper uniform," Winnie says. "Anyway, Saidi cannot afford secondary school. He only attend school one more year, until he drop out to help pay for the family." Winnie tells us what Saidi told her: he's planning to sell his reeds in the trading center all day, every day, and not only on weekends.

We're livid. None of us girls speak to Agnes the whole day. We won't let Saidi drop out in the middle of the year. At least he can finish standard eight and graduate from Mzanga Full Primary School. As soon as we're dismissed, Memory and I collect the books and march over to the trading center to find that boy.

We spot him at a metal folding table in front of the Slow but Sure Shop. A bunch of sticks lies on top of the table, and Saidi's rusty bike leans against the shop wall behind him.

"*Moni*, Saidi," Memory says. She pushes the bookmobile into the grocery store to lock up the schoolbooks until morning, when Mr. Khumala arrives early to open the shop.

Saidi smiles and waves.

"*Moni*," I say.

I'm about to launch into my sales pitch to convince Saidi to return to school, when I notice one more thing on the table. One more beautiful, amazing, delicious thing: a bowlful of cheese sticks. I almost cry when I see them. I haven't tasted one salty, cheesy stick since I arrived in this country. If there's anything that can lift my spirits, it's a handful of these. Sure, they look burned, but everyone knows that beggars can't be choosers.

"Welcome to my shop," Saidi says. "Would you like some reeds and thatching grass for your roof? Or perhaps a snack? Snack is free gift. Then you shall want to buy my reeds." He smiles.

Memory comes back outside, reaches into the bowl, and starts munching away, so I dig in too. The cheese sticks are gritty but good. "Sooo yummy!" I say, and grab another handful.

"The Glorious Blessing from America love Malawi *mphalabungu*," Saidi says.

"*Mphalabungu?*" I say with my mouth full.

"*Mphalabungu*," Memory says. "Small caterpillar from the grassland. Dried and fried!" She pops another handful into her mouth.

I chew a few more times as the news slowly squirms into my brain.

Once it does, I gag, spit, and bolt into the Slow but Sure Shop. I grab a bottle of water off the shelf, slap my *tambala* onto the counter, and run outside to swish and spit those nasty caterpillars onto the ground while Saidi and Memory buckle over laughing.

Memory can hardly catch her breath long enough to tell Saidi he needs to come back to school, and about our plan to replace the mopeds. I can't speak at all, of course, because I'm too busy trying to get every last bit of those disgusting bugs out of my mouth. As for Saidi, he manages to say, "I shall think on both of these offers with the greatest seriousness," before he erupts into hysterics yet again.

The next day after school, Patuma pushes the bookmobile to the Slow but Sure Shop while Memory and I head toward the hospital for our first day on the job.

In less than a mile, we turn off the main road down the narrow path, and it comes back to me—the night we drove here on the mopeds, the last night Innocent was alive. It was dark and I was terrified, but now everything seems so different, so calm. I glance at Memory. Her eyes are watery. I take her hand, and together we pass between the lush hills that rise like enormous green waves on both sides of the path. Everywhere we look, yellow and orange flowers explode like pom-poms while butterflies circle the thicket.

A branch rustles and Agnes runs down the path straight toward us.

Memory folds her arms across her chest. "What do you require, Agnes?"

"I require a job," she says, out of breath.

Even though Saidi still hasn't come back to school, there he is, crouched under a palm tree at the edge of the dirt lot by the hospital. He looks as peaceful and strong as ever. Memory and I glance at each other and smile. Then we wave, and Saidi joins us on the path.

"What goes on?" he asks.

Agnes slips her arm through his. "Come, Saidi. I shall work beside you. I shall be your nurse. Your uniform fit good. You are handsome like Prince Charming," she says.

"We're only working so we can replace the mopeds we took from the Chomp and Chew Stop," I say. "We're volunteering. You won't make a single *tambala*."

"It is no matter." Agnes shrugs. "I shall be most delighted to assist Doctor Saidi."

Saidi flashes a bright smile, and I can't believe it. By all appearances, he's forgiven Agnes just like that!

"Don't you get it?" I tell Agnes. "Doctor Saidi won't work *in* the hospital. Only *outside* it."

She looks at me like I'm trying to mess with her mind.

"We're painting murals. We'll work right here on the dirt." I take a deep breath. "Back in a minute," I say, stomping up the steps into the waiting room behind a man with a bloody gash in the back of his head. I'm so busy staring that I don't even notice Mr. Malola until he starts talking.

"Ahh, Clare," he says. "Wait here." A minute later, he returns with a pile of large flattened boxes that Dad and I picked up early this morning from the Slow but Sure Shop. I made certain to take only the biggest white boxes with the least writing on them so our paints would show up. Now Mr. Malola hands me two flattened boxes, and he holds the rest. Together we step outside, where he gives the cardboard to Saidi.

After we review the plan in detail, Saidi cuts out a side of one of the boxes that doesn't have anything printed on it. Then Prince Charming and Cinderella follow Mr. Malola back into the hospital to get some more supplies while I use a piece of coal that I brought to sketch. Of course, drawing when I'm furious is a serious challenge, since my hand is shaking like mad. "How can he forgive her?" I say.

"That is Saidi." Memory steps onto the edge of the cardboard to hold it down. "Always kind."

I sketch the knobby bumps of the dragonfly's body.

"Anyhow, even with high marks, most student cannot afford to attend secondary," Memory says.

I draw one of the wings and think about what she said: You have to be wealthy just to go to high school here. "You sketch the other wing," I tell Memory.

"I cannot draw," she says.

Saidi and Agnes return with buckets of water. I tell them we'll need to make purple and white paint. Then I chomp down on my pendant and watch them disappear into the forest in search of the necessary ingredients.

"Anyone can draw," Mom says. "Lie down."

"Oh, hi," I whisper.

"Now do what I say," Mom says. She explains how I should stretch out on the giant piece of cardboard and use my body to measure distance.

I lie down and place the heels of my high-tops on the tip of the dragonfly wing.

"Wow, you've grown!" Mom says.

I smile.

"You see how the length of the wing there is the same as the distance from your heel to your armpit?" she asks.

I nod.

"Now you show your sweet friend," Mom says.

I spit out the heart.

"This is how to draw?" Memory asks.

"*Inde*," I say. I sit up and hand her the piece of coal. Then I lie down on the other side of our canvas. "Now, mark the spot where you see the heel of my foot."

Memory looks at me like I'm nuts. "Go ahead," I tell her.

Slowly, she bends down and draws on the cardboard.

"Perfect!" I say, and stand. "You see how we did that? Draw the second wing here, and it will be exactly the same size as the other one."

Memory works very slowly, but when she finishes, our dragonfly looks stunning. Soon Agnes returns with a plastic bucket. African daisy petals swish in the water.

"Purple," I say, and hold out my hand. Agnes dips the rag into the bucket, then slaps it into my palm, splattering dye across our mural in all the wrong places.

"Cannot you assist with care?" Memory asks.

"You've already ruined everything!" I shout. "Maybe you'd better go. Maybe you're not needed."

"Not needed?" Agnes says. "Are you quite sure?"

"*Inde!*" Memory says.

Saidi approaches with a bucket full of cow parsley and water for the white dye, as well as a stalk of sugarcane he found out there in the bush. "Girls, my eyes surprise me," he says. "I think you are hardworking but I see I am wrong."

Of course, none of us want Saidi to think that we're lazy, so we all shut right up and grumble back to our jobs. While Memory and I fill in the wings, I force myself to imagine that the specks of purple paint on the sheet are nothing but baby insects circling the big dragonfly in the middle.

The wind whips up and a roll of thunder rumbles across the ground, so we quickly carry our creation, as well as the other boxes, into the hospital waiting room. Mr. Malola tells us he can fit everything in the supply closet since, unfortunately, it doesn't contain many supplies.

Back on the hospital porch, Saidi uses his pocketknife to cut up the sugarcane. Then we gnaw on our sweet treats and wait for the storm to stagger away.

CHAPTER 35

Agnes, Memory, and I are huddled in the schoolyard before chores debating what our next mural for the hospital will be, when Mr. Special Kingsley approaches, pressing his handkerchief against his forehead. He opens his mouth but no words come out.

"Sir?" Memory says.

Our headmaster clears his throat. "Number one, number two, and native English speaking student," he finally says, "I am most afraid I must ask a rather large and significant favor, one that shall benefit the children of Mzanga Full Primary."

Mr. Special Kingsley turns and limps away.

The three of us look at one another and shrug before we follow.

"It is a most serious matter, I am afraid," he says.

Memory shuffles ahead of Agnes and me to walk beside

him. "What is it, sir?" she asks. As we cross the school-yard, Agnes dabs her forehead with the sleeve of her dress, doing a pretty good imitation of our nervous headmaster.

"I am most reluctant to reveal that in the matter of education, the smooth fabric of carrying services to our youngsters at times becomes full of wrinkles. Those who suffer are none but our children, the individuals who deserve our greatest resources."

When Mr. Special Kingsley stops to take a breath, we find ourselves outside the standard one classroom. The hair on my arms stands at attention and I get a funny déjà vu feeling.

"It now appears that Mr. Namathaka, the teacher sent by the District Education Office, has disappeared," Mr. Special Kingsley says.

"Disappeared, sir?" Memory says.

"Yes. I am terribly afraid this is the case as it presents itself." Mr. Special Kingsley dabs his handkerchief on his forehead one more time before he continues. "Mrs. Kumwenda, the seamstress, reports that Mr. Namathaka took the minibus north yesterday after school. As he waited in front of her shop, he told Mrs. Kumwenda that the job of teaching standard one students is far too difficult. I believe he said 'too miserable.' Mr. Namathaka said he much preferred his old profession of hauling lumber up the mountainside from dawn to dusk. I believe he told Mrs. Kumwenda it was like 'sleeping in the sunshine' compared to this job."

"Sorry, sir," Memory says. "But what has this to do with us?"

Of course, I already know the answer. "I'll do it, sir," I

blurt out before my headmaster's even able to make the official request. "I'll teach English!" I say.

Mr. Special Kingsley sighs with relief. "I thank you, Clare. The children do relish the words you speak."

"Cool," I say. "In fact, supercool!"

Our headmaster turns to Agnes, who quickly stops her imitation. "There is quite a significant mountain of work to do with the exam preparation, reports to the District Education Office, as well as training our teachers," he says. "I cannot educate the children on all other subjects myself this time around. Therefore, Agnes, I think you would be most suitable to teach the maths. After all, you are smart as the bush elephant."

Agnes beams. "I thank you, sir."

"Memory, I request that you teach civics. I know this is your best subject. You might discuss geography lessons and Malawi history. I possess no doubt that the benefit to the children shall be tremendous."

"I—I do not know, sir," she says.

"I urge you most pressingly to consider," Mr. Special Kingsley says. "Please do inform me of your decision at morning assembly. I assure you, Memory, that I shall understand whether your answer brings flood or flower."

Memory nods. Then Mr. Special Kingsley turns to Agnes and me. "You two shall begin your duties tomorrow."

"I can begin today, sir!" I say.

My headmaster smiles and extends his hand toward the doorway of the standard one classroom. I reach into my backpack and pull out my scarf. I tie it around my waist, step into the classroom, and wave hello. Aneti breaks into an enormous grin. She's lost two teeth since

I've been gone. Lovemore has found a new pencil. Felicity's face looks thinner. Chikondi's belly seems fatter.

When I glance at the doorway, I still see Innocent standing in it, spreading his little arms and legs wide to keep me inside. Of course, he wouldn't have had to do that anymore. There's no place like this classroom—no place I'd rather be.

CHAPTER 36

The next week, the costumes still aren't finished, my students still don't know their lines, and we've all realized that it's true—Saidi's really not coming back to school. He refuses to return because he's making enough money selling reeds to buy a second meal each day for his family. And of course, we all miss Innocent terribly. So after school, while the standard eight girls are busy chatting on the hilltop, I decide it's as good a time as any to try out my trick that might spread some cheer.

I point to the bookmobile. "I want to show you something," I tell Patuma. "Books, please." But Patuma won't hand them over.

"I promise I won't drop them." I can hardly breathe, because what if I do drop them? There are mud puddles everywhere. The books would be destroyed.

Agnes is wearing the rainbow-striped scarf I gave her after she accepted the teaching position from Mr. Special Kingsley. "Give her a book," she orders in Chichewa.

Now Patuma looks from Agnes to me. I shrug, and reluctantly, Patuma hands one over. I try not to grimace as I set it into position. A crowd of students gathers around. "Another," I say, and hold out my hand. Agnes nods, daring me to up the stakes, and Patuma reaches into the bookmobile for one more. Soon I've got five books piled on my head.

No time like the present. I count out loud as I slowly, carefully take each step. "One . . . two . . . three . . ." I'm a tightrope walker at the circus. Out of the corner of my eye, I notice Memory approach. I try not to lose my concentration. I try not to see her flapping her arms all over the place to get me to cut it out.

I know that the turn will be the hardest part, so I hold my breath, shift my weight forward onto my toes, and pivot.

A truck's coming. I hear it. Don't see it. I wonder who it could be. Our Land Rover is usually the only vehicle around. Even the clinical officer at the hospital rides a bicycle. *Focus! Focus!* I tell myself. I take the last three steps.

"Wonderful!" Stella cries.

I pull the books down from my head and set them in the bookmobile.

"You cannot be *mzungu* from America!" Memory says, and smiles.

As I curtsy for the cheering crowd, I notice Agnes. Her mouth is wide open, like she's about to swallow the minibus that's creaking toward us.

"How goes the play?" Stella asks. "My whole family shall attend."

"It is good," Memory says. "The children think it is funny."

"It won't be funny if we don't figure out a curtain and stage," I say. "There isn't much time left at all." But none of my friends have ever heard of a curtain or a stage, so I grab my sketchbook to draw a real theater so they can see what I mean. Agnes yanks the sketchbook right out of my hand. "What is this?" she asks.

I take it back, lean against the acacia trunk, and flip to the beginning. There's the big monkey drinking a Coke that Dad and I saw on our drive to Mkumba village.

"They are such a bother!" Agnes says.

"You are such a bother!" I say, and punch her gently in the shoulder.

Agnes smirks.

"Next page," Memory says.

"Oh, no!" I say.

But my friends insist.

So I turn the pages. There are the two village musicians who face each other playing a single drum. There's the pot of *nsima* I cooked with Memory—I scrawled the recipe beside the picture. And there are a whole bunch of patterned fabrics that I've seen the ladies in the village wear. I show them all the pictures I've drawn in charcoal and ink: the elephant behind our school, the standard one students proudly holding up their letters made of termite clay, a toucan I copied from a ten-*kwacha* bill. I even show the picture of Agnes as a *bongololo*. "I was mad at you that day," I explain, and we all have a good chuckle.

When I'm through, I tuck my sketchpad back into my knapsack while Agnes clears her throat and announces, "Clare is a true scholar of Malawi culture."

"What did you say?" I ask. I can't believe she called me by my real name instead of Glorious Blessing. After Agnes repeats herself, I realize what she says is true! I really am a true scholar of Malawi culture. Of the language, money, animals. Of how the children here have fun. I do have a project to show the eighth graders back in Brookline. It's right here in my hands.

I throw my arms around Agnes. "I love you!" I say.

"Do not love me," she replies. "I am not always a nice schoolmate."

"Number two student speak the truth," Memory says.

"But Agnes is smart," I tell Memory. "So right now, I love her anyway." I squeeze Agnes again, and our other friends laugh.

"We will miss you, Glorious Blessing," Agnes says.

"Don't make me cry." I take a deep breath. I can't bear to think of leaving this place. "The show's the thing," I say. "We need to turn the Mzanga schoolyard into a real theater."

All of us sit there and think together until we come up with a brilliant plan. The most beautiful part of it is that Memory wants back in. "I must help with the play," she says. "Innocent do want me to tell the story of this chicken."

CHAPTER 37

Sickness and Patuma leave to drop off the books at the trading center, and the rest of us head to the hospital. "I must tell you that there is a boy who love me a lot," Agnes announces as we turn down the path. She plucks a sprig of cow parsley.

"What boy?" Memory asks.

Agnes twirls the stem between her hands. "The boy who left the chicken at my door on weekend," she says.

"At *your* door?" I ask. That's a big coincidence! I wonder if everyone here gets a chicken left at their door.

A man rides down the path with a very sick-looking girl slumped over on the bike rack. We press our backs against the jungle vines to allow them to pass.

"It was delicious," Agnes says, walking on.

My stomach lurches.

"I know this boy must love me a lot," she says.

"What is the name of this boy?" Memory asks her. "This boy who left you a chicken?"

"The name of this boy is Mr. Wonderful," Agnes says, and smiles. "Mr. Wonderful is a businessman. On the way to school, I see the wife of Mr. Khumala. She tell me there is a line of customer in the trading center waiting to buy his reeds. Mr. Wonderful feed his family and now me too."

Memory bursts out laughing. "This is some boy," she says. "He love Clare as well. She too did receive a chicken gift some time ago."

Agnes's brown eyes narrow to tunnels of disappointment.

"Me as well," Memory adds, and waves to Saidi, who's squatting beneath a palm tree at the edge of the hospital parking lot. "It is true. This boy love me as well. The past night I find a chicken tied to the cook-fire stone outside the hut. It did not give eggs, so Grandmother and I ate it feetfirst."

My stomach lurches for a second time. I don't think I can survive a third.

When we reach Saidi, Agnes asks him straight out: "Did you or did you not deliver a gift for a girlfriend?"

"Or girlfriends?" Memory says, and giggles.

"A gift for my girlfriends?" Saidi stands. "I do have some reeds. Or for the American girlfriend, perhaps she desire a bowl of *mphalabungu* bugs."

Memory and I laugh while Agnes turns away. But the question still clucks through my mind: if it wasn't Saidi who left us all chickens, who could it be?

The next day during our math lesson, Memory and I try to uncover the identity of Mr. Wonderful. "Perhaps

Handlebar," she whispers. "His uncle is chief of Kapoloma village and he can pay for secondary school. Did you not notice? Handlebar forever turn in his seat to search through the doorway. It is as if he longs to observe the rains." She bugs her eyes at me knowingly and giggles. "However, I think it is not the rains he watches."

Mrs. Tomasi stops writing on the board. "Chattering birds build no nests," she snaps at us. But the opportunity to gossip with Memory has stoked a flame in me—one that needs to burn.

A few minutes later, when Mrs. Tomasi is scrawling another equation, I whisper, "It could be Silvester." Silvester is skinny and small. He doesn't talk very much, and he has the longest eyelashes I've ever seen on a boy. If it's Silvester who's crushing on us, that would be cool. "You know why he's quiet?" I whisper to Memory. "Because he's keeping a secret! Isn't that cute?"

Agnes, who is still upset that her chicken isn't from Saidi, leans over and says, "Some students require advancement of studies. Please remember, some students in this classroom shall go to secondary school. After secondary school, university."

Mrs. Tomasi whips around again. She clutches the cassava chalk so tightly that it's a wonder it doesn't explode. "Girls!" she shouts. "Clean the ladies'! All of you!"

That sure shuts us up. Minutes later, our faces are screwed up with dread as the three of us trudge across the field with buckets and rags to the girls' pit latrine.

Then the day turns from awful to awfully strange: we bump right into Mr. Special Kingsley.

"You girls are role models for our young children," he

says. "You do a fine job as teachers. If you keep this commendable work going, I shall find a way to deliver a second thank-you chicken to each of you!"

I gasp.

"And where do you go with these buckets and rags?" he asks.

We role models stand there hemming and hawing until we decide the best answer to give is none at all. The pit latrines get cleaned regularly by students who have misbehaved, and we don't want Mr. Special Kingsley to know that today the honor is all ours. "Good day, sir," Memory says.

"Good day, sir," I repeat.

"Wishing you all the marvels the world can offer," Agnes adds.

Then we turn on our heels. Without another word, we march away from Mr. Special Kingsley to the girls' pit latrine, where we try to scrub our mistakes away.

CHAPTER 38

Twenty-eight days after Innocent died, it's time to mark the end of the mourning period with a ceremony called *sadaka ya lubaini*. I doubt I can handle any more crying, but of course, I go with Dad. As it turns out, all of Mkumba village is there.

Hundreds of villagers sit on the grass in a circle around a raging fire. I hug Memory and her grandmother, who are sitting in carved chairs beside the village chief. I settle down on the other side of the circle between Saidi and Dad. After the chief slaughters a goat, we all pray for Innocent's soul. Calabashes full of sweet *thobwa* made from the last stores of maize are passed around.

Memory's grandmother wears a strip of cloth around her head. She holds up a pair of khaki pants. She hands the pants to the village chief, and she unravels something else she was holding under her arm. It's a blue short-sleeved button-down shirt.

It takes me a minute to figure out what these clothes are, and when I do, my breath vanishes. It's Innocent's school uniform! Innocent's uncle Stallard lifts a clay mug full of green liquid into the air. Then he pours the muck onto the clothes. *How dare you!* I want to scream, but my vocal cords aren't working. Dad leans over. "I remember this from way back," he says. "It's a ritual cleansing. Now another boy will be allowed to wear that uniform to school."

After the chief leads a prayer in Chichewa, four men wearing white pound on their drums. And suddenly, everyone is dancing, including Memory and her grandmother. I used to think that happy people dance and sad people cry. But now I see that people aren't like stitches on a hem. They don't always follow a pattern. They don't always weave in and out, holding the pieces of their lives together in the way you might expect. Sad people can laugh and dance, and that doesn't mean they're suddenly fine. And happy people can cry, and that doesn't mean they're not okay.

It depends on the moment.

It depends on who they are in the moment.

It depends on absolutely everything.

Now Saidi, Agnes, and Dad dance along with Memory and her grandmother and most of the other villagers. I sit at the edge of the crowd, chomping on my pendant and catching salty tears on my tongue mixed with smoke from the fire. Night colors march onto the field one by one, like members of a funeral procession.

Mom's wearing a simple red dress, and she's dancing. She loves to hula, merengue, salsa. But African dancing? She's not that good. "So ask her," Mom says, out of breath.

"I can't." I hug my knees to my chest.

"Yes, you can. Your friend has been through this too many times. She is young, but she is wise," Mom says, and then she spins away from me and disappears into the waist-high field grass at the edge of the clearing.

I spend the rest of the ceremony working up my courage. I know Mom is right. Memory has traveled this path before. So, once the flames die and the dancing stops, I help Memory carry pots to the river to clean up from the feast. I've been waiting for her to ask me, but she never has. I've been wanting to tell her forever. I know it's time. Time to tell her my secret. Time to ask for hers. After all she's lost—her mother, her father, and her brother too— how does she still have the strength to wash dishes by the river? I've got to know.

"My mother died," I say.

Memory swishes the water around inside the pot with her hand. "The pot is a bother," she says, fingering the chip on the edge of the clay. She takes the rag off her shoulder and dries the pot. "I must ask Grandmother to repair."

"Memory!" I say, hurling her name across the river.

She stops and stares. "I cry every night," she says. Now it's night, so she cries. She doesn't wipe away a single tear, and there are hundreds. They *plink, plink, plink* onto the surface of the water.

"Sometimes, when I don't cry out loud, I can still hear myself cry inside," I tell her.

"Sounds like rainstorm," she croaks through her tears.

"It does," I say.

"Yet you must remember this," Memory says.

I lean forward. I must know how she does it, how she wakes up every morning, draws the water, sweeps the floor, cooks the *nsima*, goes to school. How she keeps on going when it seems impossible.

"Even the mourner must stop and laugh with the moon." She hands me the chipped pot.

"Laugh with the moon?" I lift the cloth ring off a nearby rock and put it on my head. I set the pot on top.

"*Inde*," she says. "Innocent was the sun. He is gone with my parents. Each night I watch the moon. The moon is our light in the dark. In this moonlight is the light of my family."

Memory stacks the other pots on her head. Then she grabs my hand, and together, we walk back to the hut where my father is waiting. Still waiting for me.

CHAPTER 39

We put the finishing splashes of color on a rather large ear of maize for the pneumonia ward. Then we get to work on the last mural—a mother and baby wildcat for the maternity ward. Saidi and Agnes mix the dyes while Memory and I sketch on the cardboard with charcoal. Memory has learned to draw in proportion and she's even begun to add flourishes like curly eyelashes on our cat. "Excellent detail!" I say.

She steps back and beams at her work proudly.

Then we both get down on our knees, and as we continue sketching, we talk about the play. It's less than a week away and Felicity, our new lead, still doesn't know her lines.

"I feel as if a warrior sends his spear into my belly each time I think of the play," Memory says.

"Me too," I groan.

A while later, I'm dipping a rag into the dye when I notice Mr. Malola clomping toward us across the dirt. "Clare," he says, "your daddy cannot leave the hospital at this time. He requests that you walk back to the village with your friends. He will fetch you after dusk."

Memory looks at me and we giggle, because we love hanging out together in the village at night, especially when there's dancing and drumming in the clearing for fun. So after we admire our fifth and final masterpiece for the hospital, we clean up our materials and set out on the path to the road.

Saidi announces that he'll cook us something delicious for dinner. "*Inde!* We shall feast," Memory says. "At last we can purchase the mopeds!"

"After those caterpillars, I'm not so sure I want to try Saidi's cooking," I say.

"Saidi is a man," Agnes says. "He probably cannot find the water, never mind boil—"

We stop in our tracks. Something's thrashing around in the bush at the edge of the path. Whatever it is, it's big and it's close. We hold our breath and listen to the low moan.

"Leopard?" I whisper.

"Rhino?" Memory gasps.

Saidi's eyes are wide. He pulls out his pocketknife, but I seriously doubt it will help fight a beast this large. It's only Agnes who is fearless. She pushes aside the branches with her bony hands and ventures into the unknown.

I've heard people say time can stand still, yet I never knew what they meant. But this is what happens: Time stands still. There is no short time. There is no long time.

There is no time at all, until the twigs snap and Agnes crunches back over the baby palm leaves to the path where the rest of us wait.

"*Ndi mai Kaliwo akumudzi,*" she says.

"English!" I squeak.

"There is no leopard," Agnes says. "It is Mrs. Kaliwo from Kapoloma. She was working in the fields when her baby knocked. She fell here as she walk to hospital."

"Aiii!" Mrs. Kaliwo's voice travels through the thicket to the path.

Agnes grabs Memory and me by our wrists. "We must tend to the patient," she says, and tries to pull us with her into the jungle. But I've got a better idea. "Help!" I shout. "I mean, I need to get help." I throw my backpack on the ground and sprint toward the hospital.

Seconds later I hear footsteps on the path behind me. It's Saidi. Together, we race across the lot and burst into the waiting room. Mr. Malola is nowhere in sight so we keep going, straight through the double doors.

We peek into the pneumonia ward. Five patients are hooked up to a single oxygen machine. I shudder as we run breathless inside. A nurse is checking a patient's pulse. When we tell her the news, she rushes into the hallway, and we follow.

The nurse opens a closet. Most of the shelves are bare. She grabs a pair of rubber gloves and a couple of rags, and then we're off, sprinting out of the waiting room and down the path. When I spot my backpack on the trail, I shout to the nurse to stop.

Branches scrape my legs and face as I lead the nurse into the bush, while Saidi stays on the path to give Mrs.

Kaliwo her privacy. Soon we're blocked by a jacaranda tree that's growing horizontally across the jungle floor, so I grind my foot into a knot in the wood and hoist myself up the smooth bark to the top of the trunk.

A hiccupy-pinchy sound pierces the silence.

There, many feet below me on the other side of the jacaranda tree, is Agnes. She crouches beside Mrs. Kaliwo, her face flickering in the dappled light: light and shade, shade and light. Mrs. Kaliwo's eyes are closed. Agnes takes a large leaf off the ground and fans her while Memory looks on from a few feet away.

The nurse climbs over the jacaranda trunk. She takes the baby from Mrs. Kaliwo and wipes it clean with a cloth. It's a boy! The nurse hands the baby back to his mother. Mrs. Kaliwo's eyes water as she looks at her baby. It's totally obvious that she's never seen anything so beautiful in her whole entire life. "*Timutcha* Most Miracle," Mrs. Kaliwo says, and smiles weakly.

I can't believe my ears. She just said she's going to name her baby Most Miracle. Cutest Miracle? Awesome Miracle? Rockin' Miracle? Maybe. But Most Miracle? Still, there's no way I'm going to wreck this moment with a grammar lesson.

Mrs. Kaliwo presses her lips against her baby's forehead. When she does, something inside me breaks apart, splits apart, right in the middle of my chest. I reach for my pendant. I run my hand around my whole neck. It's gone! Did it come off somewhere in the bush? Was it stolen by a branch? I need my pendant. I need my mom!

Before I know it, I'm scrambling back over the

jacaranda trunk, grabbing my knapsack from the edge of the path, and bolting away from Saidi.

"Clare!" he calls.

I can't speak.

Only run.

Run. Run. Run.

To the hospital lot, where I throw my back against the crisscross pattern of a palm tree trunk and cry.

As dusk arrives with streaks of grenadine, my mother finds me. She wraps her arm around my shoulder and plays with a strand of my hair.

"What's wrong?" she says. "Babies are beautiful."

"You're still here," I say.

"And why not?"

Maybe I've made a mistake. Maybe my necklace is in my pocket or my bag. I start to check but she takes my hands and holds them in hers. "You don't need that old thing to find me. I'm always here," she says, and touches my heart. "Now, what's on your mind?"

It's not the first time I've thought of asking her the question, just the first time I've had the guts to do it. "How did you feel when you saw me?"

"How did I feel?"

"You know. When you saw me—the very first time?"

Mom holds my chin in her hand. "I looked at you and suddenly, everything was clear—you were the reason for everything. That's why we named you Clare. For the clarity you brought to Dad and me."

"I thought you named me after your great-aunt Clara."

"Well, yes," Mom says. "That too." She touches my nose.

"And how did you feel?"

"Oh, right." Mom crosses her arms, leans back against the palm trunk, and stares into the heavens. "Okay, okay, how did I feel? I felt like the happiest woman in the world," she says.

No sooner do I sigh with relief than she changes her mind. "No, not in the world."

My heart is a hive of stinging bees.

"In the universe!" she says.

The bees fly out, dripping honey everywhere.

CHAPTER 40

Over the weekend, Dad and I follow directions to a shop in Blantyre, where Dad shells out a huge pile of Malawi *kwacha* for two extremely cool mopeds. He lets me choose the colors, so I pick out one red and one blue. The mopeds were made by the same Indian company as the ones we took, except about twenty years later. Talk about payback with interest!

While we drive all the way to the lake, we eat the sweet delicious jackfruit we bought at the market in Blantyre. "You know," Dad says, "we'll be home in a week."

"Don't remind me," I groan. Worse, the play is on Wednesday—only four days from now. When I think of it, I feel like an oxcart is trampling across my chest. Despite the fact that we've practiced every morning since I got back to school, the kids are still slamming into one another, and yesterday, when our headmaster stopped by,

Felicity was so scared she refused to speak a word until he left.

But now, as we pull up at the Chomp and Chew Stop, I know how Felicity felt. I'm so nervous I can hardly breathe, let alone speak. Dad and I wash the sticky jackfruit juice off our faces and hands with a bottle of water and an old towel that's lying in the backseat. Then we walk into the restaurant.

"Do you see him?" Dad asks.

I point to the *mzungu* who is playing cards with some locals. Everyone at the table is drinking out of coconuts with straws.

"Thought so," Dad says. He puts his hand on my back and pushes me forward.

"*Moni*, Derek," I mumble.

Derek turns around and stares. His sunburned face looks pockmarked and scary.

"It's me," I croak. But I don't think he recognizes me, so I say, "You know, the thief."

Suddenly, Derek stands and slaps my back. "Good to see you, my young friend. Your father's note mentioned the poor little chap. Bloody shame." He turns to his friends and says something about malaria in Chichewa. "Bloody shame," he says again. He lumbers over to Dad and shakes his hand. "Nice to meet you, Doctor." I think Derek's wondering if we really have the mopeds, because as he shakes Dad's hand, his eyes dart all around the restaurant.

"They're outside," Dad says. "But first, Clare would like to talk to you."

I bug my eyes out. I never said I wanted to talk to

Derek. In fact, I definitely *don't* want to talk to him. I want to leave, the sooner the better.

"A seat fer ya," Derek says. He pulls out a chair at an empty table. I sit down. Then he turns another chair backward and sits on it with his hands clasped over the back of the seat, his chin resting on them. Out of the corner of my eye, I watch Dad leave the restaurant. "Now, what's on your mind?" Derek asks me.

"It's just that . . ." I shove each word out of my mouth. "I'm really, really sorry you had to go without the mopeds for so long. I know you lost a lot of money." What I don't say is that I'm sorry I took them in the first place, because sometimes even a thief doesn't like to lie.

"You know what, Clare?" Derek presses his thumbs into the corners of his watery eyes. "You kids knew best. I thought it was heat exhaustion. If I'd believed you on the malaria, I would've driven you straight to the hospital in Machinga. And who knows? Maybe that little chap would still be here now."

CHAPTER 41

M r. Special Kingsley rings the last bell, and my classmates dash out of Mrs. Tomasi's classroom. We
meet up behind the standard five block. Together we lug
the tin roof that blew off in the storm all the way over to
the standard one class. We heave the roof on top of some
clay bricks.

"Check out our new stage!" I tell Sickness.

She grins.

"We must build large soccer goal at front of stage,"
Memory explains.

I check my watch. We've got about four hours before
the villagers arrive. After Norman takes out a pocketknife
and carves the wooden nails, we hammer the posts together with rocks. Silvester stands on Norman's shoulders
in order to get the entire goal built.

Then Memory, Agnes, and I thread a clothesline

through the curtain I made out of the extra bedsheets from the Global Health Project house. Now we secure our curtain along the top of the goalpost. The way we've set things up, our little actors will be able to walk right out of their classroom and onto the stage.

Thankfully, the field is dry and soft grass has started to grow again. Mr. Special Kingsley is busy setting torches by the edges of the field in order to keep *bongololos* and black mambas out of our theater.

At dusk, Agnes, Patuma, Sickness, and I run around the standard one room fastening hundreds of animal tails, wings, and snouts onto our little actors—costumes we made from the fabric Dad and I bought at the market in Blantyre. There was so much to sew and glue in the past few days that the standard eight girls have hardly slept at all. And now it's taking a lot longer to dress our actors than I had expected. Agnes and I need Memory's help, but we don't see her anywhere. At first we figure she's gone to the ladies', but when she still hasn't returned after a half hour, I step outside to look around.

There she is, crouching against the mud-brick wall of the standard one classroom, her head resting on her knees, tears streaming down her cheeks. I take her hand in mine. "I miss Innocent too," I say.

She nods.

"This is the story he wants to tell the world. We're making it happen. You, me, and all his little friends."

She smiles through her tears, and we pass a few minutes in silence until I ask if she can help with the hunters.

She nods again.

"All thirty-seven of them?" I hope it's not too much to

231

ask. "They each need a hat. And can you please make sure they know how to hold their bows and arrows?"

"I shall do it," she says.

As dusk sets in, the villagers arrive in droves. Inside the classroom, I clap my hands and all the creatures turn silent. I don't know if the children are excited or petrified, but for sure, I'm both. "Ten minutes till curtain!" I announce. Memory translates.

The bustle of villagers gathering in our theater makes thoughts scrape against one another in my mind until I can't really think at all anymore. I swallow and try to sound brave. "Actors, take your places!" Memory repeats my direction in Chichewa, and with the help of Agnes, the children scurry to their spots. Memory plants herself stage right. She's ready to translate the actors' English lines into Chichewa for the audience.

"One minute till curtain!" I shout. The future's in front of us. The script, the costumes, and the stage we've been dreaming of will soon become real. I glance at Memory, who smiles. I turn to Agnes, who gives me a thumbs-up. Then I peek out from behind the curtain.

Dad's sitting up front with Mrs. Bwanali, Stallard, and Memory's grandmother. Next to them are Mrs. Tomasi and Mr. Special Kingsley. Even though Saidi hasn't returned to school for classes, he's here too, just behind Dad. Alongside Saidi are Norman, Winnie, Stella, Silvester, Oscar, and Handlebar. And next to my classmates, I see the Kaliwo family. Most Miracle is strapped to his mother's back.

I take a deep breath. "Break a leg," I whisper to myself. I reach up for my pendant before I remember it's not there. "Curtain!" I call.

Agnes yanks on the clothesline.

Seven-year-old Felicity stands center stage covered in real chicken feathers Agnes and I sewed onto a pillowcase.

In the play, a chicken named Fred tries to cross the road, but she gets into all kinds of trouble. First, there are hunters who attempt to catch her. Fred escapes by flying onto the head of one of the hunters, who cannot find her there. Next there are the hyenas. The hyenas drool and lick their lips. They prepare to eat poor Fred, but when they surround her, Fred gets away by flapping her wings beneath them and tickling their bellies. The hyenas laugh so hard they start to cry. Through their tears, they cannot see where Fred has gone.

Soon Fred arrives at a large dirt road. "At last!" she exclaims. "I have found the route to safety." But when Fred attempts to cross the road, a horrible wind blows. Dirt swirls, puddles ripple, and leaves quiver. Then comes a gust of wind so strong it blows poor Fred all the way to Lake Malombe. Days later, a bunch of hippos discover our feathered heroine on an abandoned green rowboat.

"What are you doing here?" the hippos ask.

"For many months I have tried to cross the road," Fred says.

"Why do you want to cross the road?" one of the hippos asks.

Fred looks out at the audience, shrugs, and says, "To get to the other side."

Mrs. Bwanali throws her head back. Her bright sparks of laughter set the field on fire.

Before I know it, Memory and Agnes are laughing.

My classmates in the audience are laughing.

Mr. and Mrs. Kaliwo are laughing.

The children on the stage are laughing. Mr. Special Kingsley, Mrs. Tomasi, and Stallard are laughing too.

Now Dad laughs.

My mother joins in. I stare at the moon. "Hi, Mom," I *whisper.*

A giggle chimes in my ears. "Hello, Dimples!" *I say.*

A funny feeling spreads through me.

I'm laughing too.

And suddenly, I can't separate the actors from the audience, the day from the night, or the earth from the moon.

Glossary of Chichewa Words

Here are some of the words and phrases Clare learned on her trip to Malawi:

azungu (a-*zu*-ngu): white people
bongololo (*bon*-goh-lo-lo): centipede
chabwino (cha-*bwee*-no): wonderful
chonde (*choh*-nday): please
chiyendayekha (chee-yeh-nda-*yay*-kah): big monkey
inde (i-*nday*): yes
mbandakucha (m'bah-nda-*koo*-cha): early morning before
    sunrise, between first and third rooster
mbatata (*m'bah*-ta-tah): sweet potato
moni (*moh*-nee): hello
Muli bwanji? (*mu*-lee *bwan*-jee): How are you?
mvuu (m'vo'o): hippopotamus

mzanga (*m'zah*-ngah): friend
mzungu (*m'zu*-ngu): white person
Ndimakukonda (n'dim-*a-koo*-kondah): I love you
nkhuku (*n'koo*-koo): chicken
sing'anga (*sing*-ang-ah): witch doctor
sukulu (soo-*koo*-loo): school
Tiye tonse (tee-*yay toh*-nsay): Let's go
utawaleza (oo-*tah-wah*-lay-zah): rainbow
yaboo (ya-*bo*): awesome
Yendani bwino (yen-nda-*nee bwee*-no): Have a safe journey
zikomo (*zee*-ko-mo): thank you

Author's Note

The government of Malawi used to charge parents about three U.S. dollars to send their children to elementary school for a year. In one of the poorest countries on earth, those three dollars were too much for many families to afford. Then, in 1991, the Malawian government began eliminating school fees. Over the next decade, thousands of new students enrolled in free primary schools. Some aid organizations wanted to find out if the students in the schools were getting a good education.

I was sent to Malawi to help investigate. I visited ten schools. Some were urban, but most of them were deep in the bush. I found that none of the students had the materials American students routinely find in their classrooms. They certainly didn't have individual desks, overhead lights, air-conditioning, or maps. Lots of children didn't have books, paper, pens, or pencils. Many didn't even

Kids on the side of a mud road laughing in the rain. Of all the pictures I took in Malawi, this is my absolute favorite!

have the benefit of classrooms; they studied under the trees.

There were some learning materials in warehouses, but the country didn't have the resources to deliver them on a regular basis to schools in the bush. For one thing, not all of the schools were on the government-provided map, so how could the drivers find them? For another thing, the delivery trucks often lacked enough fuel to make the trips. And if they tried to go during the rainy season, often they got stuck in the mud on unpaved roads.

Despite the problems I saw in Malawi, I was incredibly impressed by how teachers and students improvised with what they did have. A few years later, when I began teaching sixth grade in Brookline, Massachusetts, I showed my students pictures of Malawian children making letters of the alphabet out of termite hill mud, and I told them how Malawian students learn fractions using pebbles.

My students had a million questions. I wanted to write a story that would allow me to share what I had discovered, but I needed help from natives of the country. Fortunately, Felicity Charity Mponda agreed to work as the first research assistant on this book. She lived in the capital city, Lilongwe, and had Internet access. She told me about her childhood: how she used to iron her dresses with hot rocks, how she yearned to be an air hostess, and how all the teenage girls wanted to be a little fat so they wouldn't look diseased. But then, at the age of forty, Felicity died.

The amazing Lovemore Nkhata became my next research assistant. Lovemore translated words into Chichewa and answered hundreds of questions about Malawian traditions, food, and education. He told me that when he was growing up, he felt that there was one good thing about not having enough paper in school: there were no written report cards! Lovemore taught me that largely because of malnutrition, twenty percent of children in Malawi die before they turn five. That's why he became a nutritionist and started a project to help prevent undernutrition in Malawian preschool children.

I was also lucky enough to talk many times with Dr. Kevin Bergman. Kevin is a family doctor in California who frequently travels to Malawi. He has seen doctors there performing surgery by the light of their cell phones. He told me that every thirty seconds a child dies of malaria somewhere in the world. That's why Kevin cofounded World Altering Medicine, a nonprofit organization dedicated to providing free life-saving medical care to patients in the developing world.

I learned a lot about Malawi from two other close friends—Stella Phiri and Norman Mbalazo—who died before their fortieth birthdays. They should have been building the future of their country. As I wrote this book, I heard their laughter in my ear and felt their spirits fill every page.

Mbatata (Sweet Potato) Biscuits

These biscuits are a common snack made by people in rural Malawi, who bake them over an open fire. My friend Lovemore says, "Eat and enjoy as we do. You will not regret it!" He is definitely right. Yum!

Ingredients
¾ cup mashed cooked sweet potato
¼ cup milk
4 tablespoons melted butter
1¼ cups sifted flour
2 teaspoons baking powder
6 tablespoons sugar, plus 2 tablespoons to sprinkle on top
½ teaspoon salt
¼ teaspoon cinnamon, plus additional ½ teaspoon to
    sprinkle on top

Directions

Preheat the oven to 375°F. Mix the sweet potatoes, milk, and melted butter and beat well. Sift together the flour, baking powder, 6 tablespoons of the sugar, the salt, and ¼ teaspoon of the cinnamon and add gradually to the sweet potato mixture. Drop by tablespoonfuls onto the greased baking sheet. Mix the additional cinnamon and sugar and sprinkle on top.

Bake for 15 minutes. OR . . .

Chill the dough for 30 minutes, then turn it onto a floured board. Knead the dough lightly, and roll it to one-half inch thick. Cut it with a greased heart-shaped cookie cutter. (Malawi is known as the Warm Heart of Africa because of the friendliness of its people.) Place the biscuits on a greased baking sheet. Mix the additional cinnamon and sugar and sprinkle it on top. Bake for 15 minutes.

Makes 20 biscuits.

Acknowledgments

People always say that writing is an isolating experience. In my case, that's not true. It took a village to write this book. Now I'd like to thank the people of my village.

First and foremost, thanks to my Malawian friends, both those who specifically helped generate many of the details in *Laugh with the Moon* and those who became friends before there ever was a book. With the greatest appreciation to my primary research assistants, Lovemore Nkhata and the late Felicity Charity Mponda. To Innocent Masaka, Oscar Mponda, Bright, the late Stella Phiri, Mercy and Stallard Mpata, and my old pal, the late Norman Mbalazo. And also to the hundreds of Malawian students, teachers, headmasters, parents, truckers, and educational administrators I interviewed all those years ago.

With tremendous appreciation to the Americans and Canadians who work in Malawi and shared their experiences and research: *Zikomo kwambiri* to Dr. Kevin Bergman, cofounder of

World Altering Medicine, who let me interview him multiple times and who read the manuscript for accuracy. To Dr. Monica Grant, Dr. Paul Hewett, Dr. Catherine Jere, Erin Mwalanda, and Krista Patrick, who answered so many questions. And also to Christina Coppolillo, who lived for years in Tanzania and shared with me the unforgettable detail of what it's like to cross paths with an elephant suffering from bad gas.

A big thank-you to the American Jewish World Service for funding my trip to Malawi and for their beautiful mission: to alleviate poverty, hunger, and disease around the world.

Next, thanks to my friends and neighbors, and to the amazing Austin writing community, especially those who critiqued the manuscript in its entirety: April Lurie, Lauren Maples and her son Bruno, and Margo Rabb. Also, Brian Anderson, Joseph Basnight, Donna Bratton, Anne Bustard, Cory Criswell, Tim Crow, Meredith Davis, Adam Duran, Chris Eboch, Lisa Eskow, Deb Gonzales, Bethany Hegedus, Varian Johnson, Dan Kraus, Cynthia and Greg Leitich-Smith, Kim McCrary, Lauren Meyers, Katie Moore, Geoff Murphy, Carmen Oliver, Andrew Perkel, Aliza Stark, Lynn Sygiel, Don Tate, Ann Walters, Rachel Webberman, Brian Yansky, and Jennifer Ziegler.

Thanks to the young readers in my life who let me bounce around ideas with them: Sarah Belin, Isaiah and Sydni Burg, and the students in the Mesquite, Texas, ISD.

Thanks to Hope Edelman for her book *Motherless Daughters*, which provided much insight into Clare Silver's journey and compared the grieving process to the cycles of the moon. And to William Kamkwamba and Brian Mealer for the compelling memoir *The Boy Who Harnessed the Wind*, which made me feel that I was right back in Malawi.

In this novel, Clare hears her mom say, "Great artists ask

great questions." My agent, Andrea Cascardi, and my editor, Michelle Poploff, are great artists, and they both asked me hundreds of extremely challenging questions in the process of writing this book. For that, I thank and treasure them. Also, thank you to Random House assistant editor Rebecca Short for her comments; to Vikki Sheatsley, who designed the book; and to Harvey Chan, who painted such an extraordinary cover! And a special thank-you to associate copy chief Colleen Fellingham and copy editor Ashley Mason for their remarkable attention to detail; and to the Random House staff who helped get this book into the hands of readers, especially Lisa Nadel, Tracy Lerner, and Adrienne Waintraub.

Finally, with great love for my family: my sister, Rachel Belin, and my brother, David Burg, who brainstormed this story with me; my parents, Sondy and Harvey Burg, who are my biggest fans and some of my best editors; my husband, Oren Rosenthal, who always gives me time to write and talks about my characters at dinner as if they're real; and my son, Rafi, who tells me funny jokes and helped choose the title *Laugh with the Moon*.

About the Author

Many years ago, Shana Burg found herself in a Land Rover in the Malawian bush, investigating whether schoolchildren had basic supplies like pens, pencils, and notebooks. Though she didn't find much in the way of supplies in the schools, Shana did make many friends. Later, as an educator and public speaker, Shana shared her experience in Malawi with her American students. She wished she could take them to Africa. With this book, she's doing just that.

Shana Burg is the award-winning author of A *Thousand Never Evers* and lives in Austin, Texas, with her husband and son.

Northern Tier Library
Pine Center
WITHDRAWN